Hidden Secrets

Anna Kuehn

Visit my website:
www.eccentrix.com/members/hiddensecrets

PublishAmerica
Baltimore

© 2003 by Anna Bess Kuehn.
All rights reserved. No part of this book may be reproduced in any form without written permission from the publishers, except by a reviewer who may quote brief passages in a review to be printed in a newspaper or magazine.

First printing

ISBN: 1-59286-175-X
PUBLISHED BY PUBLISHAMERICA BOOK PUBLISHERS
www.publishamerica.com
Baltimore

Printed in the United States of America

I dedicate this book to my one and only
Savior, Jesus Christ. For giving me
the ability and opportunity to
fulfill my dreams and become a writer.

Chapter 1

To a five year old it was a nightmare. Maggie stared blankly at her father, who was yelling back into the horrified face of her mother. It wasn't that Maggie's father was abusive to her mother. He was in fact a very loving and caring husband. Maggie never fully understood the problem. Maggie's mother, Elise Morgan, would daily complain that her father, Jacob Morgan, spent too much time with Maggie, and not enough time with Maggie's twin brother Todd.

To Maggie, Todd got most of his attention from his mother. This made up the other half of the argument. Whenever Elise would mention Maggie, Jacob would bring up Todd. It was at that point when the fighting started. Maggie and Todd would watch their parents, listening wide-eyed to what they said. At times they would stick up for each other, and when the arguing got worse they had to.

Elise Morgan grew up in Paris. Her parents were high-class social spotlights. Elise was raised to be use to all of the publics' attention. Her parents gave her the name Elise Alexandria DeVontè so the public would always recognize her. They took her to their social gatherings, showing off her creamy blond hair, and letting people marvel at the softness of her dark brown eyes. Her mother taught her how to smile so her lips would have the perfect curve and her cheeks would be lifted up ever-so-slightly. Her father hired the finest tutors, and made sure she could speak French and English fluently by the time she was ten. By entering her in national spelling bees and international geography contests, Elise's parents made sure the world knew how intelligent she really was. They raised her to be a beacon in society. The most talked about, most desired young lady in all of France.

Jacob Morgan was raised on a farm in western Massachusetts.

His father had him working on the farm the day after his first birthday. At first he would sit on his father's lap and ride with him as he plowed the fields. When he turned two his father let him feed the animals and name the baby calves. As he grew older he was allowed to do more and more.

His mother insisted that he attend a private school instead of a public one. In a class of a hundred and twenty-three students, Jacob came from the lowest class family. While everyone around him was wearing Ralph Lauren shirts and expensive slacks, Jacob wore worn jeans and faded plaid shirts. When everyone around him showed off their even tans and soft skin, Jacob was forced to hide in the background so people wouldn't see his farmer's tan and calloused skin. The kids in his class all had clean cut hairdos and in-style eye glasses. Jacob's mother cut his hair just short enough to not be long, and his father insisted he wear thick glasses to help him see the chalk board from the back of the classroom.

When Jacob was seventeen both his parents died in a train wreck. The day after the funeral he was sent to live with his aunt. There he saw how the other half of the world lived and he came to envy them. When he turned eighteen, Jacob sold the farm and went to college. He started off studying computer science, thinking there would be a future in it. But when he went two years living on the edge of nothing, Jacob went back to school and studied business. He wasn't successful until a mysterious job offer opened up in Paris. There he met Elise and the two of them moved back to America to start a family.

Because of their parents, Maggie and Todd grew up too fast. They saw too much, too soon, but they never understood it. To this day Maggie still doesn't know why her mother grabbed Todd's wrist and stormed out of the house screaming, "I should have never married you Jacob!"

River Valley, New York, was the kind of town where everyone knew everything about everyone else. Where there was never a secret kept from anyone and where you could always rely on your friends.

Although it was small, River Valley contained everything a town could need. There were two big grocery stores, and a small corner market that was only open on the weekends. A mall, which sat on Menson Street, was the main attraction for teens and young adults. Next to the mall was a line of business companies, these ranged from the local Wal-Mart to a record company store and finally finished it off with a computer company.

Because of the computer company, Menson Street was the center of the town. This particular computer company not only supplied electronic needs for the town, but also was one of the three computer bases for the United States, and one of the main representatives in the World Wide Computer Corporation. All of this was headed up by none other than Jacob Morgan himself.

Jacob was considered the most important person in the small town. He reigned over everyone, and was a well-respected citizen throughout the area. People allowed him to do whatever he wanted, whenever he wanted to do it. Jacob Morgan had the power to give a person a high positioned job, or to take one away.

"Maggie, will you please help me with my English homework?" Seventeen-year-old Delia begged over the phone.

Maggie leaned back in her computer chair and laughed. The corners of her thin lips curving upwards. "What don't you get?" She asked between her giggles.

"I don't get what's so funny." Delia protested in a jocular tone.

"Oh," Maggie caught herself, "It's not you." Pausing she added, "Now what were you saying?"

Delia let out a deep sigh, "English….homework….remember?" She reminded her.

Maggie questioned her friend again, "What don't you get about it?" Her voice almost sounded annoyed.

Delia caught on that Maggie didn't want to talk about school. "Nothing," Changing the subject she added, "so, what have you been doing lately?"

Maggie laughed again, "The same things you've been doing." She let her lips curve upwards again. Maggie leaned back in her chair and starred at a picture on her desk. It was of her and her best friend Gordon. They had known each other for almost five years, and had instantly bonded when they met. The picture was a blown-up snap-shot from the past winter when Maggie had tried to teach Gordon how to use figure skates and not hockey skates.

Delia noticed that Maggie had stopped talking. This time she asked, "What's going on between you and Gordon?"

Maggie's lips curved upwards for the third time. "Nothing." she said with a twist in her voice.

Delia knew Maggie wasn't telling the truth. "Give it up Maggie, you know he likes you."

Maggie starred at the picture, "Do you really think so?" She asked innocently.

Over the phone, Delia rolled her eyes. "Of course!" She almost yelled. "You have the perfect life."

Maggie paused before she smiled again, "That's okay, I don't want a boyfriend yet."

Delia was about say "I don't get you." When she heard the distant sound of Maggie's father in the background.

He knocked on the door of Maggie's study and stuck his head in. Jacob Morgan's dark skin and brown hair contrasted with his bright blue eyes. He smiled, "I was just checking in on you." Pausing he added, "You should probably get to bed soon, I have to leave tomorrow for a meeting."

Maggie smiled back at her father, "Okay daddy." She let her smile grow. He blew her a good night kiss and closed the door. Maggie told Delia she had to leave and waited for her to hang up.

A perfect life, Maggie thought, *if only they knew.* Maggie and her father moved around a lot. Sometimes it was because of her father's job, other times it was for different reasons that were never explained to Maggie. Currently, Maggie and her father lived in a huge, three story mansion in River Valley, New York. It was a small town that bordered a curvy river. The house was a mixture of cylinders, cones, and rectangles. Part of it was made out of stone, while the other part was a light shade of blue. In front of the house was a grand stone stairway that led to a large front door. The first floor of the house was very large in surface area, but contained only seven large rooms and two bathrooms. Maggie's study and her father's study were two of the rooms. The steps to get up to the second floor were in the back of the house in the corner of the den.

The second floor of the house was equally as big as the first floor. It contained six large bedrooms, all of which were furnished and ready to be lived in. Maggie's bedroom was on the front side of the house. The bedroom had its own private bathroom, and a large window showing a great view of the road and fields outside. The room was a dark shade of blue and had a white fluffy rug. Maggie's bed had a matching dark blue bedspread with lighter blue and white squares and circles scattered around it. It was full of fluffy pillows and stuffed animals. Her bed was on the far side of her room across from her dresser. Under her window was her desk, on which sat all of her schoolwork.

Down the hall from her bedroom was her father's bedroom. It was the largest of all the six bedrooms. It too had a private bathroom and a separate exercise room. There was another bedroom in between Maggie's and her father's room, and three more on the other side of the hall.

The third floor was smaller than the first two floors. It contained six smaller bedrooms, all of which were furnished. The third floor, however, only had two bathrooms.

Maggie turned off the light in her study and quietly went up to her room. She got ready for bed and quickly fell asleep.

The next day in school, Delia met Maggie at her locker. Delia's blond hair was worn like it always was, pulled back into a sloppy bun. She had a thin stream of bangs that would never stay where they were put. Her blue eyes and small nose made a perfect match for the welcoming smile her face showed. This made up the image of Delia Whittman, one that never changed, and could always be predicted.

Maggie's soft complexion and dark brown eyes smiled back at Delia. She tucked her brown hair behind her ears and said a quiet 'hello'. Reaching for her books Maggie said, "I'm sorry if I sounded angry last night." Maggie turned to face Delia.

Delia shrugged off Maggie's comment and joined her as she walked down the hall. After a few steps Maggie stopped walking and watched as Gordon walked up to them. His thick brown hair was was a bit messy like it was every day. Gordon's deep brown eyes were scanning the two girls he was walking up to, as his thin lips formed a slight curve. He stopped right in front of Maggie and looked down at her. After a quiet 'hello' he asked her if they were still on for that night.

Maggie smiled and nodded. The three of them stood in awkward silence until Delia broke it by asking, "What are you two doing?"

Gordon answered before Maggie could, "We're going to work on the English project together." He paused for a moment, "Do you want to join us?"

Delia hesitated, "I don't know, I don't want to intrude-"

Gordon cut her off, "You won't be." He said quickly.

Maggie saw the deeper meaning to his words and corrected him, "We'd love to have you come." She said politely.

Delia smiled and agreed that she would come. Gordon smiled back and waited for her to walk away before saying, "It's okay that she comes right?" He looked into Maggie's eyes.

Caught by the deepness of his dark eyes, Maggie waited a minute before answering. "Why wouldn't it be?"

He grinned as Maggie tried to hide the embarrassment forming on her cheeks. "Doesn't your dad have a meeting today?"

His words suddenly reminded Maggie of her father's words last night. *"I have to leave early for a meeting."* Maggie let out a disappointed sigh. "I forgot all about that," she looked up at Gordon again, "what am I going to do?"

"He won't care if we're there…will he?"

She looked down at her feet, "I don't think so, but-"

This time Gordon cut Maggie off, "It's okay, your dad's a nice guy. He won't care."

Maggie accepted Gordon's answer and started to walk towards her homeroom. Gordon easily stayed in stride with her. The two of them talked until they reached the door; there they were met by a number of other people looking to catch their attention.

Maggie had asked Gordon to stop by Delia's house on his way over so the two of them would arrive at the same time. Gordon, and his younger brother Josh, shared a car. He picked up Delia and the two of them arrived around five thirty. Maggie met them at the door and smiled as they walked in. The three of them went into the kitchen and sat down on the stools surrounding a separated part of counter. They sat in silence until Delia suggested they start their homework. Gordon and Delia picked up their backpacks and started to pull out their books. Maggie started to stand up, but when her two friends didn't move, she stopped and gave them a blank stare.

Gordon saw Maggie's confused look and spoke up, "Get your books and sit down." He said, as he patted the seat Maggie was sitting in a few moments ago.

Silently Maggie walked down to the door of her study and opened it. She entered the room just long enough to pick up her backpack. Leaving the room, she walked back down the hallway and into the kitchen where she sat down on the stool next to Gordon.

This time Delia had the confused look. "What's wrong?" She questioned Maggie on her awkward behavior.

Maggie answered bluntly, "I've never done homework at a table before," she paused, "I don't think I know how."

Gordon burst out laughing. It was a deep laugh that rose from the pit of his stomach. The laugh caught Delia by surprise and she stared at Gordon in shock.

Gordon's laugh only lasted a few seconds, he regained himself and added to Maggie's comment. Stretching his hand out so he could pull Maggie's stool closer, he placed his arm across her shoulder and said in a teasing voice, "We'll just have to teach you how."

Maggie smiled in embarrassment and looked across the table at Delia who had a content smile on her face. Maggie pulled out her English binder and opened it to her notes on the essay they had to write.

Gordon released his grip on Maggie's shoulder and followed her example by doing the same. "Any suggestions on what to write about?" He asked the two girls.

Maggie was the first to speak, "Just think about something that is important to you."

Gordon starred down at his blank paper in deep thought. Delia looked across the table at Maggie and smiled, "What are you going to write about?" She asked Maggie.

Maggie hesitated for a long moment before answering, "I think I'll write about my brother."

Both Gordon and Delia's heads turned to her in shock. "You don't have a brother-" Gordon spoke first.

Maggie interrupted him by quickly saying, "He was my twin brother, he and my mom died when I was five."

The looks of confusion were replaced by a look of pity. "Sorry." Delia muttered.

Maggie ignored her, "Anyway, I thought I would write about what he would mean to me if he were still alive."

Delia started to shake her head, "I was just going to write about my dog." She said bluntly.

Gordon looked at Delia and smiled, "I'd write about my dog, except I don't have one." He thought for a moment, "Actually, I don't have any pets."

Maggie quietly laughed at how innocent he sounded, "That's okay, I don't either."

Delia ignored Maggie and asked Gordon, "So what *will* you be writing about?"

He thought for a moment, "Probably about the family vacations we take every year."

Delia's eyes perked up in interest, "Where do you go?"

He shrugged, "Everywhere...last year we went to a small town in Nevada, and I think we are going to Salt Lake City this year..."

Maggie wasn't listening to the conversation Delia and Gordon were having. She had drifted off into the memory of when she and her father had lived in Nevada. Those were the worst years of her life, and she hated it when she remembered them. *I just wish I had a normal family like Gordon,* she told herself, *or at least a normal father.*

Jacob Morgan was far from a normal father. He let Maggie do whatever she wanted, and never really cared if she did anything without his knowing. He wasn't a bad father, but he was always consumed in his work. Maggie loved the times when he would spend days with her and they would go out and do things together, but when he had his business meetings and was consumed in his work Maggie learned to be more of a business alliance than a daughter.

People always told Maggie that she was lucky to have a father like him. They said she got everything she wanted, and she never had to worry about not being allowed to do anything. Most people saw Maggie as the girl that got away with the world, and Maggie hated it. Only a few people knew Maggie for who she really was, an innocent girl trying to hide her life from people so they wouldn't make assumptions.

"Maggie..." Gordon pulled her back to reality.

She looked up at him with a blank stare.

"What are some of the places you've gone on vacations?" He asked.

Delia spoke up before she could answer. "Yeah, having a dad with that much money, I bet you've gone everywhere."

Maggie winced, she hated it when people brought up her father's financial status. It was true that Mr. Morgan was very well off, but Maggie hated all the memories that were connected to that money.

Maggie answered the question shyly, "Once my dad had a business meeting in Maui and he took me with him. But I stayed at the hotel beach the whole time. So I guess it wasn't much of a vacation."

Gordon's eyes widened in amazement, "So you've really never been on a vacation?"

She shrugged, "I guess not."

Later that night, after Delia had gone home, Gordon and Maggie were talking on Maggie's back porch. Maggie was sitting on the edge of the railing, and Gordon stood facing her. The setting sun made the sky a dark shade of purple mixed with a light shade of blue. The large orange sun barely showed over the horizon.

Gordon smiled as he stared at the sunset. "Isn't it amazing?" His words drifted off into the fading sunset.

Maggie turned herself around so her back was to Gordon. She watched as the sun faded slowly, "Gorgeous." She whispered.

Grinning, Gordon took a step forward and let his hands gently rest on Maggie's shoulders. She smiled and let herself relax underneath his grip. Maggie leaned back and let her head rest on his chest. Gordon's grin grew. Stepping another step closer, he moved his hands down her arms and held onto both of her hands. He rested his chin on the top of her head. Neither of them said anything as they starred into the setting sun. After a few minutes Maggie broke the silence.

"Gordon-"

He interrupted her by saying, "I want you to come over tomorrow. My mom has been dying to see you again." He slowly backed away as Maggie started to turn around to face him.

Looking up at him, Maggie smiled. "I'd love to, but I want to spend some time with my dad, so can I wait until later in the day?"

He laughed, "Of course."

Chapter 2

Maggie came into school late the next day. She didn't tell anyone why, she just handed a note to the attendance office that said she and her father had been dealing with business. The woman at the desk accepted the note simply because nobody in River Valley ever questioned the dealings of Jacob Morgan.

She walked into her fifth period class, handed the teacher her green slip, and quietly sat down. Gordon looked at her questioning, but she quickly looked away, trying to hide the small tear that was forming in the corner of her eye.

Gordon noticed the tear and questioned her about it after class. "Is something wrong?" His deep brown eyes looked intently into hers.

Maggie didn't say anything, she let herself be captured by the embrace of his stare.

Gordon saw the sadness in her eyes. Quietly he asked again, "What's wrong Maggie?"

Maggie's voice cracked as she talked, "It's...it's nothing...really."

Gordon wasn't convinced, but he wasn't going to argue either. He simply nodded and asked her if she was still coming to his house that afternoon. Gordon was surprised by her answer.

"Can I come directly after school, or are you busy?"

He gave her a welcoming smile, "Sure, you can ride home with Josh and me."

Josh was Gordon's younger brother. He was a year younger than Gordon and was a junior that year. He and Gordon looked a lot alike, the two of them would almost pass for twins if Josh didn't have light blue eyes. Gordon's older brother was two years older than he and was in his first year of college. He lived at the college and only came home on weekends.

Maggie was still acting unusual when Gordon met her at her locker that afternoon. He smiled and waited silently for her to get her books out of her locker. After a few moments the two of them started to walk towards the door. Gordon tried to start a conversation between them.

"How was your day?" He asked as he looked over at her.

Maggie answered vaguely, "It was okay."

Gordon got her hint and stopped asking questions. The two of them walked silently out into the parking lot. Gordon led Maggie to where the car was parked. They got in and waited a few minutes before Josh opened the back door and climbed in.

He greeted Maggie with a pleased smile. Patting her on the shoulder he asked her how she had been.

Hiding her true emotions Maggie answered, "Good…you?"

He smiled and agreed that he had been good as well. Gordon put the key in the ignition and started the car. They drove and turned at the corner. After driving down the road for a few moments, Gordon turned into the driveway of a medium sized white house. It had a small front porch and a light blue front door. There were matching light blue shutters on all of the front windows.

The three of them got out of the car. Josh held the door open for Maggie and Gordon to walk through, and then disappeared into the living room as soon as Mrs. Allister, his mother, came out of the kitchen to greet Maggie.

"I thought I heard your voice." She said cheerfully as she smiled at Maggie. Mrs. Allister's curly blond hair bounced on her head.

"Hello Mrs. Allister." Maggie said, equally as cheerful.

"I am so glad Gordon finally invited you over again, I was beginning to miss that lovely smile of yours."

The corners of Maggie's lips curved upwards.

"That's the one I was talking about." She paused, "I have to tend to dinner, you will be staying, won't you?"

Maggie's smile grew, "Only if you want me to." She answered politely.

Janet Allister shook her finger at Maggie, "You better not miss it." She said with a large smile on her face. With that, Mrs. Allister turned and walked back into the kitchen.

Maggie turned to Gordon, her expression had changed and was now very serious. "Gordon," she hesitated, "I have to tell you something."

He grinned and looked at their surroundings. "Right here?"

She shook her head and started to walk towards the stairs. Gordon followed her up the steps and into his room. Maggie sat down on his bed. Gordon's small room was a mess. Clothes were thrown on his bed and all over his floor, and there were papers and food wrappers scattered about. Gordon shut his door and pulled up a chair so he was facing Maggie. Leaning his elbows on his knees he waited for her to speak.

Maggie was silent for a long moment. In her head she was trying to figure out how she was going to tell him. Finally she spoke, "It's about why I was late this morning."

That much Gordon had already figured out, but he didn't say anything.

"Around six o'clock this morning," she started, "a guy came to our house. He was from the Investigational Team of Paris. He had information for my dad about my mom."

This time Gordon did say something, "I thought your mom had died?"

She looked down. "That's what I told you, and everyone else." Looking back up she added, "I lied because I didn't want to face the truth."

"About what?" Gordon looked confused.

Maggie saw his confused look and realized that she would have to tell him the whole story. "I guess I should tell you about my brother."

Gordon gave her a blank stare until he realized that Maggie had told him about her brother last night. He changed his expression and told her to continue.

"He didn't die either. He's my twin brother, his name is Todd." Maggie watched as Gordon slowly processed this information. "When I was four my parents started fighting. I don't know what it was about, but I remember my mom always telling me she hated me." Maggie's face showed the pain she was feeling. "Shortly after we turned five my parents got in a huge fight. My mom kept saying she should have never married my father. The only part of that night I remember was when she grabbed my brothers wrist and said she was moving back to Paris."

Gordon caught her eyes in his stare. When he was sure he had her full attention he asked, "What did the guy say this morning?"

A small tear started to form in the corner of her eye. "He said that a week ago my mom and brother were in a fatal car accident. My brother was fine. He just had a broken arm and a lot of bruises, but my mom suffered from a major head injury and a lot of blood loss. She died the next morning. He came over to tell us that my dad would have to go pick Todd up from a holding house he was staying at. That's why I wanted to come over here right after school. I don't want to be alone anymore." The tear that was forming slowly started to run down her cheek.

Gordon reached out his hand and caught her tear with his thumb. He let his large hand rest just under her cheek as he looked deeply into her eyes. "Maggie, do you remember your mom?"

She slowly shook her head. "Only the times when they were fighting and the night she moved away."

Gordon moved his hand off her cheek and grabbed her hand. "If you really don't remember her, then it shouldn't be that bad, should it?"

Maggie thought for a long moment. "I don't know. She was still my mom, but I didn't know who she was. All those times I told people she was dead, to me she really wasn't alive." Maggie's voice drifted off as if she was trying to remember something. When she spoke again, her voice was almost a whisper. "I just wish I had a normal family, and a normal father that wasn't hiding things from me."

Gordon lifted his eyebrows, "There's more?" He asked curiously.

Maggie nodded, "My father tried to hide my brother and mom from me completely. He married another woman and they had a son, he hoped I was too young to remember that she really wasn't my mom. Those were the years we lived in Nevada and his plan would have worked except those were the worst years of my life and I remember them like yesterday."

Gordon stood up and sat next to Maggie on his bed. He reached his arm behind Maggie and held her shoulder firmly. "You know what?" He questioned her. "If your life was any different, you wouldn't be the same Maggie that you are now." Gordon tried to cheer her up.

Maggie looked up at him and smiled, "I'm just afraid to see Todd tonight."

"What do you remember about him?"

Maggie looked up at the ceiling. She smiled and remembered her brother. "He had the darkest brown hair I've ever seen. He had blue eyes, and a short oval face, with the cutest cheeks. He was always laughing, like he had the world going for him." She looked back at Gordon, "He's a lot like you."

Gordon ignored her comment and asked about her other brother. "What's he like?"

Maggie sighed, "I don't like talking about him, but I guess you deserve to know." She paused, "His name is Kevin. Right after my parents divorced, my father and I moved to a house in Nevada. It was a nice house, and my dad had a good business going. One night after school I came home and there was this tall red head sitting with my father on the couch. My dad turned around and told me they were getting married. I ran out of the room and didn't talk to him for days. When I finally did he told me that she was pregnant and I was going to have a little brother."

Gordon didn't know what to say. He waited for Maggie to continue.

"Nine months later they had a kid and named him Kevin. After about a year my father had this job offer in New York City. He insisted on taking the job, but his wife didn't want to go, so he took me and left. A few weeks later they signed the divorce papers and he was single again."

Gordon was shocked at how Maggie took divorce so lightly. "Doesn't that bother you?"

Maggie turned so she was facing Gordon. She leaned against the headboard of his bed and crossed her arms over her stomach. While changing her position she asked, "What? That my father left the woman I hate? No." She watched as Gordon's eyes widened, lowering her voice she added, "What bothers me is that my mom left us all those years ago and my father never did anything about it."

Gordon nodded in understanding. The two of them sat in silence for a few minutes. Finally Maggie had enough courage to ask, "Gordon, will you come with me when I go home tonight?"

He looked deeply into her eyes one more time. "Sure." He said with a smile on his lips.

The two of them talked for a while longer before going downstairs to join the rest of Gordon's family. They ate dinner and conversed with his family for the rest of the night. Around nine o'clock Maggie said she should probably go home. Gordon asked her if she wanted him to drive her, but she said she would rather walk.

The two of them walked to Maggie's house. When they arrived, Maggie's father's car was already in the driveway.

"Do you think he'll be worried?" Gordon asked, hinting that Mr. Morgan might not have known where Maggie had gone.

Maggie quickly shook her head as she walked up the steps. "No, I told him I'd be at your house." After a quick pause she added, "Will you come in with me?"

Without saying a word Gordon walked up the steps. He held open the door and followed her in. As they walked down the hallway, Maggie's heart started to beat harder.

When they turned into the living area, Maggie stopped. Standing only five feet away was a medium height young man. His right arm was in a sling. He had his dark brown hair brushed forward, hints of yesterday's gel still showed on some parts. His hair was thin, with some strands of it hanging down over his forehead. He was wearing baggy blue jeans and a baggy black shirt that had a red circle in the middle of it. He had blue eyes, and a smooth nose. His lips were thin, and straight. He wasn't smiling or frowning, it almost looked like he was biting his bottom lip.

Nobody said anything, their thoughts just hung in the air. Finally after staring at each other for what seemed to be minutes, Todd spoke. His voice was deep, but still had a ring to it. He spoke in a slight French accent from living there for so many years. All he said was, "Maggie?"

Chapter 3

Maggie stood there, astonished. *This is Todd, he's really here.* These thoughts kept flowing through her head. Maggie didn't know what to say.

Todd walked up to her. "It's good to see you again." He laughed, "Are you just going to stand there, or are you going to say something?"

Maggie caught herself starring at him, "Sorry." Was all she could manage to say.

Todd lifted an eyebrow, the expression made Maggie laugh. "Whatever." He said. Pointing his head towards Gordon he asked, "Who's this?"

Maggie caught herself again, "Oh, I forgot." Gordon smiled at Maggie. "This is Gordon." Gordon kept his smile and looked at Todd. Sticking his hand out, Gordon realized that Todd had a cast on his right arm and he pulled his hand back. Todd shrugged it off and grinned.

"Nice to meet you." His French accent rang throughout the silent house.

Gordon nodded and commented that he should probably get going. Turning to Maggie he looked deeply into her eyes one more time before completely turning around and walking out the door. As soon as he left Todd spoke again.

"Nice guy…is he your-"

Maggie cut him off, "Friend."

Todd grinned, "Oh, I get it." He said with a twist to his voice.

Maggie looked around the room before walking over to the couch. "Where's dad?" She asked.

Todd followed her and sat down on the opposite end of the same couch. "In his office. He got an important phone call and has been in there ever since."

Maggie tried to force a smile, "That's dad for you."

Todd ignored her comment, "I guess I should start with all the questions I have." He said politely. "What's...River Valley like?"

Maggie laughed, "Basically it's a small town where everyone knows everything about everyone else."

Todd began to shake his head, "Far cry from Paris."

"Sorry Todd, but it's probably not as exciting either."

"Okay, so if the town is that boring, what do you do all day?"

Maggie smiled, "You go to school, which isn't that bad. The people are pretty nice and most of the teachers are okay. And we're seniors this year, so we get away with everything. After school you either go home and hang out there, or you go to Menson Street. It's the center of the town, everything you do is centrally located there."

Todd nodded as he took all of this information in, "So..." He started, "...tell me some more about school."

Maggie answered Todd's questions for a little less than an hour. After a lot of talking she decided it was Todd's turn to speak. "Do you speak fluent French?" She let her curiosity flow out.

Todd leaned back his head and laughed, "Of course." He paused and added, "I learned it along side of English, but I think I know French better because that's all I really ever spoke."

Maggie's interest continued, "Did all your friends speak English?"

He shook his head, "Most of them were learning it, but they only knew a few phases."

Maggie waited a moment before asking the next question. "What was mom like?"

Todd didn't say anything, he sat there and thought for along time. When he finally spoke it was in a quiet voice. "I don't know how to explain her, everything she did had purpose, and she always had everything planned out." He paused, "After the divorce she became a famous dress designer, it was like that was the only thing she ever did."

Maggie was listening intently, "Did you see her a lot?"

He shook his head, "Sometimes she was gone for weeks at a time, but it never really bothered me."

Maggie didn't respond.

"So what are the people like around here?" Todd asked changing the subject.

Maggie looked up, glad to be off the subject of her mother. "They're pretty nice." Maggie grinned, "I'll have to introduce you to Delia."

"Who's that?" He questioned.

"Just a friend. She'll think you're the coolest guy ever, besides Gordon. I don't know what you'll think of her though."

Todd shook his head, "I can't wait to see her." He said sarcastically.

Maggie smiled, "You'll more than likely be treated like a god." She told him, changing the subject off of Delia.

Todd questioned her on what she meant by that.

"Because of dad's high position in the town, everyone treats him like a celebrity." She smiled, "That means that we get treated as celebrities too."

Todd grinned, "Sounds fun, is it?"

Maggie shook her head and laughed, "No, I hate it. Everyone thinks I have such an easy life, and they treat me like I get everything I want, when I really don't. I just wish they would leave me alone and treat me like a normal person."

Todd nodded in understanding. "What about Gordon?" He asked, "Where does he fit into all of this?"

Maggie knew the answer right away, but she didn't let on. "Gordon has a weird way of choosing his friends. A lot of people like him because of his morals and because he's such a nice guy. But he doesn't let it get to his head."

Todd lifted his eyebrows, "Everybody likes Gordon?" He asked doubtfully.

Maggie shook her head, "You'll always have your group of people who think he is old fashioned and nerdy. They're jerks to him."

Todd nodded and thought for a moment. "What about that Delia girl you mentioned?"

It was six when Maggie woke up. There was a knock on her door, it opened and Todd walked in. He was smiling. After taking a shower, getting cleaned up, and fixing his hair, he looked pretty good. His only fault was his cast that went over his elbow, and the dark blue sling that held it up.

Maggie stumbled out of bed, she spoke in a tired voice. "It's too early to be up." She mumbled at her brother who was now searching thought the drawers of her desk.

His smile grew bigger. "Get up." He said bluntly. Turning to her he added, "Dad said you keep extra folders and notebooks in your desk. Where are they?"

Maggie started to shake her head as Todd searched through another drawer. "They're in the desk in my study. I'll get them for you later." Pausing she added, "Now leave so I can get dressed."

Todd grinned and walked out of her room. Maggie took a quick shower and did her hair. She tied the laces on her white shoes and jogged down the steps into the den. Smiling at the familiar scent of her father's pancakes, Maggie walked into the kitchen and sat down next to her brother. Moments later her father placed a plate of pancakes in front of her. She looked up and smiled, "Thanks dad."

He smiled back and sat down across from his children. "I called the school this morning," Maggie and Todd both waited to hear what he had to say. "They said Todd could start today as long as they received all of his information by the end of the day." He turned to Todd, "So I need the name of your old school so I can call them and have them fax everything."

Todd nodded and told Jacob the name of his school. "Good," He started again, "You two will just have to stop by the principals office before you go to homeroom to get Todd's schedule."

Both of the teenagers nodded and finished eating their breakfast. Maggie went into her study and found a few folders for Todd to use. She handed them to him and he went back up into his room. Maggie called him down a few minutes later and he walked down with one of the backpacks he had brought over. The two of them got in Jacob's car and he drove them to school.

Chapter 4

Maggie and Todd arrived at River Valley High School a few minutes later. They walked into the building and turned right down the hallway. After passing two closed doors, Maggie turned into the doorway of the first open door. On top of the door was a sign that read 'High School Office'. Maggie confidently walked up to the front desk and smiled at the secretary.

She smiled back, "What can I do for you Miss. Morgan?" She said in a soft voice. Her grayish blond hair curled under her ears.

"Hello Mrs. Cordina." Maggie said politely. She turned and looked at Todd, who was standing a few feet next to her. "This is my twin brother Todd, he's just moved here and my father told us that arrangements have been made to allow him to attend school today." Maggie spoke very professionally as she smiled down at the secretary.

Mrs. Cordina looked extremely confused, but Maggie didn't feel she needed a better explanation. The stout woman sitting at her desk slowly pushed the intercom button that connected to the principal's office. She explained the issue to him and waited for him to respond. He immediately asked the secretary to lead both Morgans to his office. She stood up and walked over to his door. When she reached it, Mrs. Cordina held open the door and waited for the two Morgans to walk through.

On the other side of the door was a tall, stout bald man. He was wearing a black suit and a dark blue tie. His fat lips were in a straight line, showing that he wasn't pleased with having another Morgan attend his school. As soon as they sat down, the principal, Mr. Gonseena, spoke. "I understand this is your brother?" He pointed the question towards Maggie.

She nodded.

His outstretched arm reached for a memo that was sitting on the edge of his desk. "I received this a few minutes ago. All it says is, 'Todd Morgan-make quick schedule'. I understand your father's position Maggie, but I can't let Todd into school without all the proper information."

Before Maggie could defend herself Todd spoke up. "Sir," Mr. Gonseena gave Todd a thin-eyed glare. "my father will have all of the information needed faxed to you by the end of the day."

Mr. Gonseena continued to glare at him, "By the end of the day?" He contemplated, "How do I know I can trust you?"

Todd grinned. Without saying a word he slightly stood up and reached into the back pocket of his baggy blue jeans. He pulled out a small, black, padded case. Opening the flap on the front he pulled out a cell phone and offered it to the tall man in front of him. "If you would like to call him and confirm it-?"

Mr. Gonseena motioned for him to put his phone away and tried to ignore the subject. "I'm sure you're right." He suddenly sounded worried. Reaching into the top drawer of his desk he pulled out a green slip of paper. He jotted down a quick note on the back of it and handed the slip to Todd. "Just show this to all of your teachers." Reaching into his desk one more time, the principal pulled out a manila folder. Inside were only two papers. One of them he handed to Todd. It was his schedule. He quickly shut the folder before either of the teenagers could get a look at what the other paper was.

He motioned for both of them to leave the room. When they were back in the hallway Todd asked, "Why did he suddenly change his attitude?"

Maggie smiled, "He knows the power of a Morgan. When you challenged him he was suddenly reminded of it."

Todd gave her a confused glance.

She explained, "Dad's business is spread nation-wide, but he still controls a lot of little companies. One of his biggest things is funding small businesses that open up. He likes it because he then owns the business until they can pay him back. That never happens, so dad has dibs in half of this town's businesses."

Todd gave her another confused look, "How did the school get involved in that?"

Maggie laughed, "Last year the budget for school didn't pass. Dad is on the board, and instead of cutting the programs at school, he insisted that he donate the money. Because he donated such a large amount he has earned the respect of everyone employed by the school." She paused as they turned the corner again and walked past a long row of lockers. Maggie pointed to a locker by a small group of guys. They walked over to it. "So dad has a big say on most of the jobs at the school. A lot of times they come to him and ask him whether or not to hire or fire somebody."

Todd nodded as he read the combination on his schedule. He gave the lock a quick pull and opened the door. The space inside was empty and small. Todd opened his backpack and threw all of his folders into it. Turning to Maggie he asked, "What do I need for each class?"

Maggie explained to him what he should take to each of the classes on his list. While she was explaining Gordon came up from behind her and surprised her by putting his arm around her shoulder. He gave it a quick squeeze and let his arm fall to his side. Maggie smiled and looked up at him. "Hi."

He smiled back and said hello to Todd. Gordon walked with them until a tall blond boy called his name. Maggie and Todd left him and continued to walk down the hallway. They turned into the last doorway before the hallway stopped. Standing next to the door was a well-built, handsome man. Maggie smiled at him and introduced her brother.

"This is my brother Todd." She said to the teacher, "This is Mr. Sunus." She told Todd.

Todd reached into his pocket and pulled out his green slip. He handed it to Mr. Sunus and waited for him to read it. After a few moments the teacher handed the slip back to Todd and nodded. "Cool." He said in a deep voice. The three of them lingered for a moment before Mr. Sunus added, "What happened to your arm?"

Todd hesitated, "A car accident." He said carefully.

Mr. Sunus shook his head. He looked behind Maggie and Todd to where another student was waiting to talk to him. He excused himself and let Maggie and Todd go on their way.

Maggie hadn't walked two steps when Delia rushed up to her. She didn't say anything at first. For a moment she looked between Todd and Maggie with a confused look on her face. Finally Todd smiled at the blond girl that was standing in front of him. "Todd." he said, "Todd Morgan."

Delia's eyes widened, "Maggie-".

Maggie interrupted her, "Delia, meet my twin brother Todd."

Delia gave Maggie a confused look, "Maggie," She hesitated, "you told me he was…" Delia tried not to sound blunt. "…dead."

Todd instantly burst out laughing. Delia gave him a deadly stare. "Don't laugh at me. That's what she said." She insisted.

Todd was taken back by Delia's harsh tone. He stepped back and lifted his left hand up in a surrender. "Whatever you say." He said, trying to avoid the subject.

Delia waited a minute before asking, "What did you do to your arm?"

Todd looked down at his right thumb. He was silent for a long moment before answering. "It was a car accident."

Maggie slowly slipped away and was shortly joined by Gordon who had just entered the room.

"Ouch," Delia continued, "did it hurt?"

Todd laughed, "Yeah it hurt." He answered as if to imply it was a stupid question.

Delia caught the tone of his voice and changed the subject. "Where did you move from?"

"Paris." He said quickly.

"Why?" She questioned him.

He hesitated and was going to say "legal reasons", but instead Todd just shrugged and turned to join Maggie and Gordon at the front of the room. Delia followed him and sat in her normal seat next to Maggie. The moment she sat down a voice came over the loud speaker telling everyone to stand for the pledge of allegiance. Todd stood awkwardly and listened as everyone around him was saying, "I pledge allegiance to the flag of the United States of America, and to the Republic for which it stands, one nation under God, indivisible, with liberty and justice for all.".

The voice came back on and instructed everyone to sit for the morning announcements. The room went silent as all of the students and the teacher listened to the principals deep voice tell them what was going on that day.

Chapter 5

The bell rang for first period and everyone stood up to leave. Maggie pointed Todd in the direction of the math room. He walked out into the hall and tried to find his way around the swarms of people trying to get to first period. He watched as people looked at him with a question in their eyes. Todd ignored them and kept walking. *No one in this school is friendly.* He thought to himself. Todd looked up at the door number on the room Maggie had pointed too. *121, I think this is it.* Todd turned into the doorway and looked around for the teacher. He was standing on one side of the room writing an assignment on the chalkboard. Todd walked up to him and got his attention.

"Excuse me, are you the math teacher?" He asked politely.

The teacher turned around to see a medium height brown haired boy that he had never seen before. Slowly he nodded, "Is there something you need?" He asked in an unsure voice.

Todd reached into his pocket and pulled out the small green piece of paper the principal had given him. He handed it to the teacher and waited for an answer.

The teacher read the short note, and looked back at Todd. "Todd Morgan? Are you related to Maggie Morgan?" He asked.

Todd nodded, "Twin brother."

The teacher smiled and stuck out his hand, "I'm Mr. Hobley, I teach math. If you just hang on for a few moments I'll get you a book, and show you where you can sit." Mr. Hobley walked over to a tall cabinet on the other side of the room, opened it and picked up a book from one of the piles. He then walked back over to where Todd was standing and handed him the book. Todd muttered a quiet thanks. Mr. Hobley looked around the room, "I think the only open seat is that one in the back." He said as he pointed to a seat that was excluded from the majority of the class. It was in the far left corner of the back row, and it appeared to be surrounded by a group of giggling girls. Todd sighed and walked over to his new seat.

As he placed his books down on his desk he got the attention of the group of girls. The loudest one, who seemed to be in charge of everything, spoke up first. "Are you new here?" She asked in a high voice.

Todd sat down, slouching in his chair, "It appears to be that way." He said in a depressed voice.

She looked at him closely, "Why are you so down?" She asked him.

Todd looked up, slightly surprised by her concern. She was a short girl with long blond hair. She didn't appear to be very skinny, but Todd didn't think she was very fat either. He shrugged, "I don't particularly want to be here."

She laughed, "None of us do." The girl paused for a moment, and then added, "My name is Kailey...Kailey Borger, what's yours?"

"Todd Morgan." He said quietly.

The girl's eyes perked up, "Are you Maggie's brother?" She asked energetically.

He nodded.

"That is so cool!" She nearly screamed. She was about to say more but was interrupted by the teacher wanting to start his lesson.

By second period most of the grade had already found out that there was a new kid and that he was Maggie's twin brother. As Todd walked into the art room he was greeted by a group of people. Everyone was asking him questions about where he was from and why he came to their small town. Todd didn't answer any questions, he just walked up to the teacher and handed him his green slip of paper. This teacher seemed a lot nicer than the last one, and Todd found him easier to explain things to.

"I'm Mr. Katcher." The teacher said as he extended his left hand.

Todd shook his hand, and told him his name. Mr. Katcher said he had already heard it, and explained to Todd how fast moving the grapevine of this school was.

"One question," Mr. Katcher started, "why did you come over from Paris, I would think you would want to stay there."

Todd thought of how he could answer his question. He didn't want to give a harsh answer, or tell the teacher to back off, but he didn't think he could explain to everyone about his mother. "Custody reasons." Todd answered, hoping the teacher would get the hint, and not ask him any more questions on the subject.

Mr. Katcher nodded. He turned around and picked up a sketchbook from behind his computer. He handed it to Todd and told him he could sit wherever he wanted to. Todd thanked him and turned around. The class was divided into seven groups of four desks. All but two seats were filled up, one was in a group of girls, who appeared to be giggling, and talking while they starred at Todd. He looked over at the other open seat, it was with a group of guys, one of them was normal aged, and appeared pretty short, the other two looked older than the rest of the class. One of them was talking to a blond haired girl in tight fitting clothes. She looked up as Todd started walking that way. Stepping away from the guy she was talking to she walked up to Todd and started to ask him questions. "Your name's Todd isn't it?"

He nodded, another two girls walked over and stood in front of Todd.

The blond continued to talk, "Where did you come from?" She asked him.

He sighed, "Paris." Todd tried to walk forward but the growing group of people around him would not allow it.

Another person spoke up, "How come Maggie never told us about you?"

He shrugged, "Ask her."

The questions were flowing in, and Todd tried to answer them in the vaguest form he could think of. He was about to plow his way through everyone when a deep voice told everyone to back off. "Give him some room," he said, "You'd think he was an alien or something." As the people started to back away one of the older looking guys from the group Todd was walking to stuck out his hand and introduced himself. "Kevin Jacobs," he said.

Todd attempted to shake his hand, "Todd Morgan." He replied.

Kevin nodded, "I know, you're Maggie's brother. That's cool." He started to say. He motioned for Todd to sit down in their group, then sitting back down in his seat, Kevin introduced Todd to his friends. "This is Drake Frane," he said pointing to a well built, blond haired guy. "That's Josh Ginley." He said as he motioned towards the shorter, younger looking guy.

Josh smiled, "How do you like being the talk of the school?" He asked Todd.

Todd sighed, "I hate it." He said bluntly.

Josh lifted his eyebrows, "Really...I think it would be fun."

Kevin shook his head, "When you live a life of publicity, you tend to hate every minute of it."

Josh looked back at Todd for affirmation, Todd nodded, impressed with what Kevin knew.

Josh looked back at Kevin, "How did you know he lives in publicity?"

Kevin laughed, "He's a Morgan." After a brief pause he added, "His dad is the lead computer representative of the United States and holds monthly business meetings with twelve of the most important people in the computer world. I'm sure his mom does something extraordinary too."

Drake finally joined their conversation. "What does your mom do?" He asked Todd.

Todd looked down. "She was a famous clothes designer in Paris." He said in a quieter tone.

Josh looked confused, "Was?" He asked.

This time Todd looked up. "Yeah, she died a few days ago."

The three other guys didn't say anything.

When the bell rang to end second period Todd had to ask directions on how to get to the French room. He stopped by his locker to pick up a different set of folders, and then walked up the stairs onto the second floor. Josh had said the room was the first door on the right.

This classroom was set up differently than all the other rooms. The desks were lined up in long rows, each end of the row connecting to another end. With all the desks put together it was a square missing one side. The teacher's desk was in the middle of the side without any desks. It was facing all the other desks, and had a chalkboard behind it. The French teacher was standing next to the chalkboard writing words and their translations in a long list. Todd smiled, knowing he would ace this class.

He walked up the teacher and handed her his green slip of paper. She read it, and introduced herself as Mrs. Fay. He took the book she handed him and sat down in the seat she assigned to him. The bell rang shortly after and the class began.

Mrs. Fay took order immediately. Todd noticed how no one in the class was really paying attention, he silently thought about how stupid they all were. *French is the best language.* He told himself.

Mrs. Fay started to talk, "You are all in your third year of French by now, so I expect you to be able to talk in complete sentences. Can anyone give me a sentence they know in French."

No one in the room raised their hands, most of them were slouching in their seats not listening at all. Todd slowly raised his hand.

The attention of the class suddenly turned to Todd. "Yes, Todd. It's nice to have a new student participating in class." Mrs. Fay told him.

Todd spoke in fluent French, not messing one word up. "*Qu'est-ce que voulez-vous que je dise? Je sais meilleur Français que l'anglais.*" A grin formed on the corners of Todd's lips. He hadn't spoken French in days, and it made him feel good to speak the language he loved.

The teacher's eyebrows grew in amazement, as did the rest of the class. "I did not know you spoke fluent French Todd."

He spoke again. "*êtes-vous venus de Paris, que prévoyes-vous?*"

A huge smile formed on the lips of Mrs. Fay, she smiled and played alone, trying hard to make her sentences as fluent as Todd's. *"Projetez-vous sur participer réellement á la classe, ou allez-vous tomber journalieren sommeil?"* She stumbled with some of the words.

Todd laughed, *"Je pense que je pourrais prêter l'attention."*

Mrs. Fay smiled in satisfaction, *"Bon."*

On his way to the social room Kailey Borger confronted Todd, "I didn't know you spoke French." She told him.

He laughed, "I grew up in Paris, French became my first language."

Kailey smiled, "That is so cool." She paused for a moment, "Do you think you could help me with my French homework sometime?"

He shook his head, "I think if you paid attention in class you might learn something."

Kailey took his comment offensively, "I pay attention." She told him.

He shook his head again, "No one in that class does…you guys were all daydreaming."

"What are we suppose to do? French is such a boring language," She asked him.

Todd looked down at her, his eyebrows raised, "French is not boring, it's so…" He tried to think of the right word. "…classy."

Kailey broke out laughing. "You're too funny." She told him as he turned the corner, and walked into the social room.

Mr. Sunus was in the same happy mood during fourth period that he was in during homeroom, and Todd found him to be a really good teacher. Some of the things he talked about Todd had never heard of before, but he found it very easy to catch on. Todd decided he would ask Mr. Sunus about the things that he didn't understand some other time. One of the things Todd noticed when the class first started was Mr. Sunus didn't just teach social studies. He came up with ways for the class to interact with the lesson so the students would actually experience some of the things that happened in history.

After social studies Todd went to lunch. He met Maggie by her locker and told her how his day had been going so far. She laughed at some parts, and felt bad for him as he told her about the others. When he was done talking she told him about the hundreds of questions she had gotten during the day about her brother.

"Maggie," Todd started, "why does everyone think it is so cool that I am your brother?"

Maggie laughed, "I don't know…but after you've lived with me for more than a week you probably won't think its any fun at all."

Todd was quiet for a moment, suddenly he thought of something Kevin had said to him earlier. He asked, "So dad really is treated like a celebrity around here?" Last night when Maggie had told him that he didn't believe her, but now he was beginning to wonder.

Maggie nodded, "Everywhere we go." She said confidently. "People just don't get it…he's rich, he doesn't need on-the-house meals every time he wants to eat out."

Todd laughed, "That's awesome."

Gordon walked up to meet them, "Maggie!" He shouted, "You'll never guess what happened!"

She smiled, "What happened?" She asked him, knowing it wasn't anything too important.

He shrugged, "Nothing. I just like to get overly excited…it puts perk in my day." He started to laugh as Maggie shook her head.

Maggie, Todd, and Gordon met Delia in the lunchroom. The four of them sat down at a round table and started to eat their lunches. A few moments later a tall, dark blond haired boy walked over to their table and sat across from Maggie. As soon as he sat down he yelled out Maggie's name, "Maggie!" He screamed. Maggie looked up and smiled, she yelled back. "Chris!"

Maggie and Chris had become friends instantly when they first met last year. Ever since then they would always yell out the other persons name whenever they saw each other. It wouldn't matter if they were in the hallway, or walking into a classroom. Out of tradition, when Chris saw Todd he instantaneously yelled out Todd's name too. "Todd!" He screamed.

Todd's head shot up, there was a startled look in his eyes. "What?"

He asked, a sound of annoyance in his voice.

Chris smiled, "Are you going to be okay?" He asked Todd.

Todd shook his head, "I'm sorry..." A slow smile formed on his lips, "No, I don't think I am." He finally said.

Chris tried to give him a sympathetic look but ended up wearing an awkward smile, "I know what you're going through." He said, trying to at least sound sympathetic.

Maggie started to laugh, Chris looked at her, his deep blue eyes shining. "How come you never told me you had a brother?"

She didn't have time to answer before Delia butted in and answered for her, "I'm sure it's the same good reason as to why she didn't tell me either."

Not very long after Chris had joined them, people started to form a crowd around Todd. Maggie, Gordon and Chris found it humorous, but Todd saw it differently. He kept answering the same questions, and giving everyone the same looks. By the end of the twenty minutes they had to eat, he was more than ready to leave lunch and get on with his day.

For fifth period all four teenagers had English. Everyone in the class except for Todd handed in their writing assignment, and everyone was given another sheet of paper explaining their next writing assignment.

Mrs. Gray, the English teacher, stood in front of the class and gave instructions. "It would be a lot to ask all of you to write a fiction short story about a made up characters life. However, for the states expectations you have to do something along that line. In front of you is the description for your next assignment. You and a partner have to come up with a story line, give me all the characters names, and their roles in the story. You then have to create some kind of chart, or graph showing how all the characters interact with each other." She waited for everyone to settle down again, "On Wednesday next week you and your partner will have to come up in front of the class and give a presentation. You can present your story line in any way you would like, as long as it is appropriate."

Maggie raised her hand.

"Yes Maggie?" The teacher asked.

"How many characters do we have to have in it?" Maggie questioned.

"You can have no more than three main characters, and you have to have at least two minor characters." She looked around to see if there were anymore questions. Seeing that there were none, Mrs. Gray told the class they could get started.

Maggie got up and sat next to Delia, while Gordon moved over next to Todd.

"Maggie, I hope you know what you're doing, because I haven't got the slightest idea." Delia pulled out a piece of paper and wrote on the top, 'step one: clueless'

Maggie laughed, "This is going to be easy, all we have to do is come up with a name, and a face. Put a little personality into this person, and graph him or her on a chart. Trust me, things just start coming to you." Maggie smiled.

Gordon was listening in on Maggie. He walked up behind her and whispered in her ear, "Would you please share some of this knowledge, I'm lost too." He smiled.

Maggie turned to him and laughed, "It's not that hard you guys. Why don't the four of us get together today after school? We can work on it then."

Gordon nodded and looked at Delia, "Okay with me, what about you?"

Delia looked at Maggie, and back at Gordon, "Sure."

"Cool," Gordon said, and went back to his seat.

Delia looked like she was going to burst. "Maggie I love you!" She nearly screamed.

"No really Deal, that's okay, you don't have to..." she thought for a moment. "What did I do now?"

"I get to go to your house again! But this time it's with Gordon and Todd."

Maggie shook her head. "Deal, none of them are that great. Sure they're nice guys, but..." Maggie caught herself, she couldn't think of anything to say.

Delia caught on. "You know you like him Mag." She smiled, "Just admit it."

Maggie thought for a moment. "He's just really nice, that's all, we're just really good friends." Maggie took the piece of paper from Delia and wrote, 'step two: torment partner.'

Todd put down his pencil, and faced Gordon, "There's something I've been wanting to ask you about Maggie." He asked as he looked over at her a few desks away.

This caught Gordon's attention, he looked up, "What?"

"Is she…" he chose his words carefully. "…stuck up?"

Gordon looked shocked, "Maggie? No, she's one of the most modest people I know. Why do you ask?"

Todd looked down at his paper again. "Someone told me today that Maggie always had the easy way out, and nothing bad ever happened to her."

Gordon shook his head, "Don't listen to whoever told you that…" He paused for a moment, "Maggie moved here when she was thirteen, that's when I met her. She doesn't talk much about her life before that, but I know that it wasn't pleasant. Trust me, Maggie's been through some horrible things."

Todd closed his eyes and remembered, everything suddenly came back to him again. *"I hate you!" His mother screamed, "I always will! You stupid child, get out of my way!" Todd's mother slapped Maggie across the face, her nails leaving four deep scratch marks on Maggie's right cheek. Todd was watching from the corner, his mother didn't know he was there. As soon as Maggie was hit he ran out and took Maggie's arm, he pulled her away, running up the steps and into his bedroom where he hugged Maggie and tried to stop her from crying. "It will be okay." He told her, again and again. "It won't happen again." Todd spoke those words to Maggie constantly, but they never came true. Everyday their mother would say something horrible to Maggie, but today was worse. This time it left a mark, and their father would find out soon. He would march downstairs and confront his wife about her abusive acts. They would fight into the night, and when they were finally done their father would come upstairs and check on Maggie. This night was different, Maggie didn't stop crying because of the deep scratches on her cheeks. Todd tried as hard as he could to calm her down. He knew if she was too loud their mother would come up and make things worse.* Todd opened his eyes and looked over at Maggie. He didn't know if she remembered the night or not. The two of them were only four, but Todd remembered it clearly.

Gordon's face was filled with concern, "Are you okay?" He asked Todd, bringing his attention back to the present.

Todd looked up, after a moment he said, "Yeah, I just…just got lost in my thoughts." He tried to change the subject. "One more question."

Gordon lost some of the concern in his face, "What?"

"You and Maggie, what's the deal there?"

Gordon grinned, "Already playing the role of big brother?" He asked, "I'm going to have to get use to that."

"No really, what's the deal between you two?"

Gordon shrugged and looked down, "I don't know, she likes to think that we are just 'good friends', but someday it'll be more than that."

Todd smiled, "Does she know you like her?" he said bluntly.

Gordon looked up and then smiled at Todd's bluntness. "If she does, she's not letting on."

Chapter 6

At the end of the day Gordon met Maggie at her locker. Maggie was getting her books from her locker and putting them in her backpack. He reached down and picked up her backpack, holding it in midair for her. Maggie finished putting her books in it and closed it up. She then took it back from him and put it over her shoulders.

"Thanks." Maggie told him.

Gordon smiled, "Are Delia and Todd coming?" He asked her.

Maggie looked past Gordon and saw Delia walking down the hall next to Todd. Delia was enjoying herself immensely, and had a huge smile on her face.

Gordon noticed Maggie was looking behind him and turned around. He quietly waited for the two of them to catch up with Maggie and himself.

After the four had gotten their things they headed out of the building, as they walked to Maggie and Todd's house they talked. Maggie and Todd were talking about the past, while Delia and Gordon listened intently.

"Maggie, after me and mom left, what did you and dad do?"

Maggie shifted her backpack. "A few days after dad packed everything up and moved out, I'm not sure exactly where we went…I think it was somewhere in Nevada. We stayed there for a few years and then moved to New York City. When I was thirteen we moved here."

Todd looked over at Gordon. "How did you and Gordon meet?"

Gordon butted in, looking over at Maggie he said, "On Maggie's first day of school in seventh grade she got completely lost, and dropped her books everywhere. I picked them up for her, and showed her where she was supposed to go. We've been friends ever since."

Maggie smiled at the memory, "He wouldn't leave me alone for the rest of the day…it was so much fun."

Gordon looked intently at Maggie, "You actually had fun that day?"

Maggie nodded, "No one had ever been that nice to me before."

Todd took a deep breath in, *"I hate you!" "I'll always hate you!"* He tried to snap out of it, but he couldn't, *"You stupid child!"*

Delia noticed something was wrong with Todd, "Are you okay?" She asked him.

He was finally able to focus on the present, "Yeah." He told her, regaining himself. Todd changed the subject, "When did you meet Maggie?" He asked Delia.

"I think it was the same day," Delia started. "Maggie was in almost all my classes, and we just became friends. She invited me over to her house one night, and we had a blast. It was the best, but then Maggie and Gordon became really close, and they have completely forgotten about me."

Gordon laughed, "We never forgot about you, the first time I ever tried to do something alone with Maggie, she wouldn't come because she was afraid you would hate her for life."

Maggie got defensive, "When was this?" She looked over at Gordon, smiling.

Gordon grinned, "It's not important."

Maggie looked over at Todd, a curious look on her face, "What did you and mom do when you got to Paris?"

Todd thought for a moment, "Mom got a house, and started the business she had left back up, not very long after she became one of the most famous dress designers in France."

The four continued to talk as they walked to the Morgan house, filling each other in with details they had missed in life, and basically just having a good time. When they got there the four of them went to the kitchen and helped themselves to everything that was in the fridge. When they had stocked up on enough food, they took it all and went into Maggie's study. Gordon instantly sat down on the same couch as Maggie and left Todd and Delia to sit in either of the two plush chairs.

For the first few minutes everyone ate their food in silence. Todd was looking around studying the features of the room as he took chips from the bag and put them in his mouth. Delia kept stealing the bag of chips back from him so she could get her share. Gordon was eating a nutty buddy while he silently watched Maggie sip her iced tea.

Maggie was the one who broke the silence, "Do you guys want to work on English now?"

Gordon popped up, "Sure," he said energetically. He picked up his backpack, and pulled out an orange folder. "Todd, did you think of any ideas?" he asked.

Todd looked up, "No, I was thinking the main character should be a boy." He said with a boyish grin on his face.

Maggie started to laugh. "Great Todd, I was beginning to wonder how far you had gotten." Maggie joked. "What about you Deal, how far have you gotten?"

Delia gave a childish smile. "I think our character should be a girl!" She said energetically.

Gordon walked over to the now standing Maggie. He placed his arm around her shoulder and said, "I don't know Mag, maybe we should let them do their own thing while we work together. I'm in the mood for a *good* grade." The two laughed.

This time Todd got up. "Are you saying that I can't write?" He asked sarcastically.

Gordon let his head back in a pretend laugh. "Never, what made you think that?"

Delia got up and joined the conversation. Standing next to Todd she said, "Oh Todd, give it up, Maggie is the best writer, we all know it."

Todd slowly turned to Delia, "You really think that?" He asked her.

She nodded intently.

"Okay, you're on, the team with the highest score on this

assignment wins."

Delia stood closer to him, staring in a competitive way. "Wins what?" She challenged.

Todd leaned forward, making their faces only a few inches away. He grinned, "The right to brag."

Delia stepped back and smiled. As if it was planned she looked over at Gordon who had pulled his arm off Maggie's shoulder. A cry for help shone in his eyes, "No, Todd, you don't know what you are up against...I don't want to have to put up with these two when they beat me in something!" He pleaded with Todd to take back the bet, but Todd refused. He held a look of confidence in his eyes.

"Don't be so negative, Gordon, we'll whip them." He gave Maggie a competitive look. "Let's go, we have to get to work." He pulled Gordon to one side of the study. Delia and Maggie worked around the computer, and at the computer desk.

"I have this brilliant idea." Maggie whispered, moving closer to Delia.

Delia lifted her eyebrows in anticipation.

"Okay, we have this character, a girl. She lives a normal life, in a middle class family. She goes to a public school where everyone likes this one popular guy. He'll be our second main character." Maggie stopped for a moment. "Are you with me so far?"

Delia nodded, "Yeah, girl, boy. I got it."

Maggie smiled, "Anyways, the parents of the popular guy figure out they have a daughter. They find out who it is, and it's the one girl. Her parents don't want to give up their adopted child, so the case goes to court, and it is decided that this girl will live with her birth parents on weekends."

Delia asked, "What does the girl think of all this?"

"She doesn't know." Maggie continued, "She doesn't like this guy like most people, she became friends with him and got to know him. This made her figure out that he really isn't as great as people say he is. The only problem is I don't know what could happen next." Maggie looked over at Delia for help.

Delia thought for a moment. "How about, we come up with

something that happens to the guys parents, like they get killed or something. They find out later in the story that they really didn't get killed, they faked it so these terrorists wouldn't kill them or something."

Maggie's eyes lit up. "That's good, but terrorists wouldn't be after any ordinary person. We'll have to put them in a high position."

Delia nodded, "We could make him president, that way it's even cooler that she is his younger sister."

Maggie lifted her eyebrows, "I like it."

Delia smiled, "Lets get to work."

"Gordon, I've been thinking," Todd started, "and I have this great idea."

Gordon looked up at him, "What?"

"Okay, there's this guy, he's lived in an orphanage for his whole life, his parents died when he was little. According to the state that he lives in, when you turn eighteen the orphanage gives you a certain amount of money, and says you can leave."

Gordon nodded, "I'm with you so far."

"Well," Todd continued, "This particular guy couldn't wait to get out of there, so when they gave him the money he was gone, but he didn't know what to do. He had never really lived in the outside world. He ends up in the mall, and this one girl finds him, he was sitting on a bench, in ragged clothes, and she feels bad for him. She walks up and talks to him. When she hears his 'life story' she really feels bad for him. She calls her father up and asks him if this boy can stay with their family until he finds a job. The dad says that he can, but he'll have to work for him at his business."

Gordon kept nodding.

"They boy accepts, but the girl says that if he is going to work for her father, he'll have to have some decent clothes. He tells her he only has this certain amount of money. She says she'll buy everything, and he can repay her later on in life."

"I'm with you so far, but what's the dilemma in this, everything is going so good?"

Todd answered, "The two become close friends, the only problem is the girl's boyfriend. He is really controlling, and doesn't like it when his girlfriend talks to other guys."

Gordon nodded, "I get it, so how are we going to end this?"

"She dumps her boyfriend for this really nice guy, and they become best friends for life." Todd smiled.

Gordon nodded again, "I like it, but Todd, do you realize who we are up against?"

Todd shook his head, "I have no idea how Maggie writes, but I do know how I write." He grinned.

Gordon gave him a confusing look. "You write well?" He asked.

Todd shrugged, "It must run in the family. But they didn't want to send me to a writing college for having a heritage." Todd laughed at the memory.

Gordon lifted his eyebrows in amazement. "Cool, have you ever had anything published?"

Todd shook his head, "This one poem won a contest, but that was a long time ago. I actually like to keep my writing to myself, it's not a normal guy thing to be writing all the time."

Gordon nodded in understanding. "Let's get to work."

The two teams worked into the afternoon, Maggie and Delia had already started their presentation, while Gordon was trying to keep up with the fast working Todd. Every idea Gordon would come up with, Todd would add to it, or form another idea off of it. Gordon was constantly trying to come up with brighter ideas so Todd wouldn't think he was completely stupid.

Gordon looked over at Todd, shaking his head. "You just don't appreciate my abilities." Todd looked up and laughed. Gordon hadn't realized it, but Maggie had walked over, and was standing behind him.

"I know Gordon, we just don't appreciate you. I'm so sorry." She spoke with fake pity.

Gordon turned to her and smiled. Twisting backwards in his chair,

"All the great things I do for you, and look how you treat me."

Maggie smiled. She placed both her hands on his cheeks, and shook his head, "You poor baby." Maggie turned and walked away, leaving Gordon starring after her.

Todd shook his head and laughed.

Gordon looked over at him, "What?" He asked.

Todd just shook his head again, "You two are so cute together. It's actually really funny."

Gordon looked over at Maggie, then at Delia. "You should get to know Delia better, *you two* would be really cute together."

Todd shook his head, "Maggie said something like that, but I don't like that whole girlfriend/boyfriend scenario."

Gordon smiled, "Maggie told me the exact same thing a few weeks ago."

Todd gave him an interesting look. "Why did she tell you that?" He asked.

Gordon didn't say anything, he just looked down at his paper and grinned. He looked back up and shook his head, "It's not important."

Chapter 7

Gordon and Delia left not long after Mr. Morgan came home from his daily rounds. Jacob ordered a pizza and sat down to talk with his children.

"How was your first day?" He asked Todd.

Todd thought for minute, thinking of the best way to describe his day. "It was okay. French was fun…but I kept getting asked the same questions all day."

Mr. Morgan's eyebrows went up in interest. "What kind of questions?"

"Where are you from? How come Maggie never told me about you? Why did you come over from Paris? Are you really Maggie's brother? This list goes on."

Maggie laughed, "He didn't get half the bickering I got."

Jacob looked over at his daughter, "What happened to you?"

"Everyone wants to come over to my house because they think my brother is so hot." She told her father bluntly.

Her father let out a hearty laugh. "I think it must run in the family." He said with a twist in his voice. Jacob Morgan had the same dark brown hair and bright blue eyes as Todd. To all the unmarried women in the town he was the most eligible bachelor.

Jacob's two children laughed along with him. The humor went on into the night. The pizza arrived and Mr. Morgan passed it out to his children. As he was passing out the pizza a thought came to his mind, "Todd, I called for some of your things to be sent over, so if there is anything else you want just tell me and I'll get it."

Todd tried to thank his father but his mouth was full of pizza and only a few muffled noises came out of his mouth.

After Maggie and Todd went to bed that night, Mr. Morgan went into his office and sat down at his desk. He glanced down at his watch. *11:28, good it's not too late where she lives.* He told himself. He picked up the phone and dialed a number for a house in Nevada.

A woman answered the phone. "Hello?" She asked in an exhausted voice.

"Samantha?" He asked her.

"Yes," her voice livened up, "who is this."

"It's Jacob." Mr. Morgan replied.

"Jacob!" She said in a surprised voice. "It's been years…why are you calling?"

He ignored her question, "How have you been?"

The next day in school went the same as the day before. There weren't as many questions, but people still looked at Todd in the same way, and people still asked Maggie why they had never been told about her brother. Todd's favorite classes quickly became art and French. He took Gordon's advice, and started to talk to Delia more. Maggie invited her over on Saturday and Todd started to become fond of her free nature.

Maggie and Delia were making cookies while Todd was sitting down at the kitchen table watching them. Delia looked back at him while Maggie was opening the butter. "Come help us." She told him in a playful voice.

He smiled and reluctantly got up from his slouching position. He walked over and stood next to Delia, Maggie leaned forward and saw him. She smiled and handed him the wrapper from the butter.

"Go throw this out." She told him.

He obeyed and walked back to his previous position. When he got back Delia was trying to measure out a cup of sugar. Maggie was holding the measuring cup over the bowl while Delia poured the sugar into it. The two of them were laughing when most of the sugar missed the measuring cup and landed in the bowl.

"My cookies will never be the same as Mrs. Allister's." She said while shaking her head.

Todd looked up, "Who's that?"

Delia answered, "Gordon's mom."

Todd nodded, "Oh."

Delia put down the bag of sugar and allowed Maggie to dump the measurement of sugar into the bowl. Turning to Todd, Delia asked, "Can you get three eggs?"

He silently obliged, walking over to the fridge he opened it and skillfully balanced three eggs in his one hand. Carefully walking them over to Delia he handed them to her. Todd watched her as she took them from his hand.

Maggie turned on the beater and started to beat all the wet ingredients together. Delia added the bowl of dry ingredients and patiently waited for Maggie to finish beating. As soon as she was done Todd walked over and stuck his finger into the dough. He scooped out a small finger-full and licked his finger clean. Delia shook her head.

He saw her and asked, "What...the dough is the best part."

She agreed, "But we haven't put the chocolate chips in yet."

As if on cue, Maggie opened a bag of chocolate chips and dumped them into the mixture. Using a wooden spoon she mixed them so they were evenly distributed throughout the dough. This time Delia stuck her finger in and licked it clean. She turned to Todd, "It tastes better *with* the chocolate."

He was about to taste the dough again when Delia said, "You can't use the same finger...that's disgusting."

"I don't have another finger." He said defensively.

Delia picked up Todd's good hand. "You have four other fingers that you could use." She told him.

Using his middle finger, Todd tried another taste of the cookie dough. He agreed with Delia that it tasted better with the chocolate. Maggie found some cookie sheets and the three of them started to bake the cookies.

Chapter 8

The week went by quickly. All the questions Todd had been asked earlier that week started to fade away. Numerous girls asked Todd to the Senior Fall Ball, but he declined them all saying he wasn't going with anyone because of his arm. Delia was disappointed when she heard this, but was even more surprised when Todd called her that Thursday night.

She answered the phone, "Hello?"

Todd spoke, a slight sound of nervousness in his voice. "Delia?" He asked.

Delia didn't recognize the voice. "Yeah, who is this?"

"Todd."

Her heart skipped a beat, "Hi." She said, now in a slightly perkier voice.

Todd smiled from the other end of the line. "This is really going to sound weird, so bear with me."

It was Delia's turn to smile. "Okay." She told him.

"I'd ask you to come to the dance with me, but because of my arm I'm not going to be doing much dancing. So I was wondering if, on Saturday, you might want to get together and do something?"

Delia was treasuring every word Todd spoke. "Will Maggie and Gordon be coming too?" She asked, expecting him to say yes.

"No," He said, "I think Maggie is going to go to his house in the morning. I don't know how long she is going to be there."

Delia answered his question for him, "Probably all day, those two are funny like that."

Todd sounded confused, "What do you mean?"

"Maggie and Gordon could spend weeks together and never get

bored. Sometimes they'll just talk for hours and still have things to talk about when they are done. I just don't get it."

"If I hear one more word out of you I swear I will kill you!" Maggie's mother screamed. She stormed out of the room, leaving Maggie sitting on the couch holding her mouth with her hand, a small tear running down her cheek. Todd closed his eyes, he had been watching from the steps, as soon as his mother had left the room he ran down and sat next to Maggie, telling her that their mother wasn't serious and that no one was going to kill her.

Todd tried to change the subject, "Oh, so do you want to get together?" He asked, getting back to his original point.

Delia got excited, "Sure." She answered, trying to hide her excitement.

The two of them talked for a few more minutes. Delia finally told Todd she had to go and hung up. Todd put down the phone and fell onto his bed. "I can't take this anymore." He told himself. Todd closed his eyes and slowly drifted off into sleep.

Friday night, the night of the dance had come. Around six o'clock the four friends walked back to the school. When they first got there, nobody did much of anything. Finally Gordon took Maggie's hand and led her out to the dance floor. They danced for three songs straight not taking a break, only stopping momentarily between songs.

Todd looked over at Delia, "What's the deal with Gordon and Maggie?" He asked. The sound of music in the background made it so Delia had to move closer to Todd to talk to him.

Stepping closer to him she said, "They do this at every dance. They would dance the whole night if they could." Delia smiled at Todd, who had turned his attention to her.

Todd looked confused, "Why?"

Delia took a breath, "Okay, Maggie loves dancing, she always has. When they first met, Gordon asked her to the middle school dance. They both went, and had a great time, but the problem was Gordon wasn't a very good dancer. Maggie told him that if he stepped on her foot one more time, she would never dance with him again."

Todd nodded, a smirk growing on his face.

"The next morning, Gordon went over to Maggie's house and asked for lessons."

Todd lifted his eyebrows in amusement.

"The two went upstairs and danced for half the day, only taking a break for lunch. It was amazing. Now at every dance, Maggie and Gordon dance the whole night, only stopping once or twice for a drink."

Todd gave Delia a funny look, "So they actually come to dances to dance?"

She nodded.

Todd asked, "Do you?" He had a grin on his face.

Delia shrugged her shoulders.

Todd frowned and looked down at his cast. "I'd ask you to dance, but I don't think I could."

Delia noticed he was looking down at his cast. "That's okay."

Todd looked up at Delia, "Are you thirsty?" He asked her.

"Kinda."

He smiled, "I'll be right back." Todd walked over to the drink table and poured two drinks. He feebly attempted to carry two drinks with one arm.

On his way back Delia walked up to him and took one from him. "I could have gotten them." She told him.

He shook his head, "That wouldn't be right, the guy is suppose to do things for the girl."

Delia was charmed, "You're the old-fashion type aren't you?"

He nodded shyly.

Delia's smile grew bigger, "That's cool."

"Really?" He asked her. Todd had always been use to girls thinking it was dorky, or stupid that he acted the way he did.

"Yeah, not too many people are like that. I think it's cool."

"Good."

Delia looked down at his cast, "Is that the first time you've broken something?" She asked Todd.

He laughed, "No, definitely not the first."

"What else have you broken?" Delia asked curiously.

Todd grinned, "When I was five, and we first moved to France, I fell down the steps at my new house and broke my wrist. When I was seven, I went mountain climbing. I was almost to the top when I lost my grip. The rope swung me around and I hit the side of the mountain. I kept falling, luckily there was a little edge that I landed on, but I broke my leg, and dislocated my elbow."

Delia cringed. "Ouch."

Todd smiled and continued, "When I was ten I was roller skating on a half-pike and lost my balance at the top. I slid down and broke my other leg." Todd laughed at the memory.

"Is that all, or is there more?" Delia asked.

"One more," Todd started, "when I was fifteen we went on vacation to Hawaii, I had taken surfing lessons and I thought I had it down, but I hit the wave at the wrong time and it flew me through the air. I would have been okay, but my surf board came with me and hit my arm at the perfect angle, breaking it."

Delia shook her head, "That's why I don't do things that risk my health."

Todd looked back at his cast, and then at Delia again, "Someday I'll take you somewhere, and you'll get hurt."

"I don't want that to happen." She complained.

He grinned, "No, no, no, I'll come and save you."

Delia laughed, "As long as you save me."

Todd smiled, whispering loud enough so only Delia could hear what he said, "Don't worry, I will."

Gordon looked into Maggie's eyes. The two didn't realize that their feet were moving, or that one would turn, or step aside at some time.

Maggie smiled, not sure of what to say. For the first time in her life she was speechless around Gordon. He grinned, and took her hand as the next step in the dance. Maggie let go of his hand, and wrapped her arms around his neck. She stepped closer to him as he wrapped his arms around her slim waist.

Gordon's grin turned into a smile, while his eyes were still locked onto hers. Maggie opened her mouth to say something, but Gordon placed his index finger slightly on her lips, silencing her.

Maggie scanned his face for an explanation. He didn't show any, still gazing into her eyes. Maggie tried to smile, but found it hard. She realized then how nervous she was. Her heart started to pound harder, and she felt lightheaded.

Gordon began to notice something, "Are you okay?" He asked, a concerned look on his face.

Maggie looked up into his caring eyes. "Yeah," She forced a smile, "do you want to take a break?" She asked, stopping in the middle of a step.

Gordon looked confused, but he wasn't going to argue. "Sure," He walked next to Maggie to the set of chairs along the wall. They sat down, Gordon looked over at her, a very concerned look on his face. "What's wrong?" Gordon reached his hand out and grabbed Maggie's, holding it tight in his.

Maggie shook her head, not realizing that there was a look of fear in her eyes.

Gordon didn't have to ask to know something wasn't right. "Do you want to go talk about it?"

Maggie realized she would have to tell him. "Yeah, but not in here."

He stood up, pulling Maggie up with him, "Okay." They started to walk towards the gym door. In the hallway, a door was open that led to the outside, letting the cool air rush through the hallway.

The coolness of the outside air hit Maggie. She finally realized what was happening. They walked closer to the door, the only light was coming from a small exit sign above the door.

Gordon faced Maggie, a caring look in his eyes. "What's wrong?" He looked slightly confused.

Maggie took a deep breath, prepared to tell him everything. "We're friends right?" She asked.

He nodded, "Of course." He said, not sure of where the conversation was going.

"Gordon..." she looked into his eyes. "...How close are we?"

He expected her to say that. "I don't know," Gordon thought for a moment. "It all depends on you."

Maggie didn't know what he meant. "Why?" She asked him.

Gordon reached both his hands out and took both of hers. "Because...If you want us to be closer, that we can. But if you don't, I'll leave you alone for a while. I just don't know how to act around you."

Maggie was blunt with him. "Gordon, I think I like you...a lot more than just a friend."

A huge smile started formed on his lips, "You have no idea how long I've been waiting for you to say that."

Maggie smiled. Letting her curiosity take the best of her, she asked, "How long?"

He grinned. "Too long."

Maggie laced her fingers through his, stepping closer she asked. "Does that mean you like me too?"

His grin grew bigger, "Since that day in seventh grade when I picked up your books."

"Really?"

He nodded.

"How come you never told me?"

He looked down, "I was afraid you'd think I was crazy."

She shook her head, her smile growing.

Gordon smiled, listening to the faint sound of music in the background he said, "Maggie, we're missing our song."

Without saying a word, the two quickened their pace, and headed back toward the gym. When they reached the door Gordon opened it for Maggie and followed her in. The two stepped right onto the dance floor and started to dance. This time filled with a newfound enthusiasm as they stared into the other person's eyes.

Chapter 9

A cold breeze flew across Maggie's face and brushed through her hair. Walking against the wind she shivered. Maggie let the sleeves of her hooded sweatshirt fall over her hands to warm them. Turning into a paved driveway, Maggie quickly walked up to the front door and knocked on it.

She saw Gordon through the long glass door. He turned when she knocked, and smiled when he let her in. After she was inside he questioned her, "What brings you here on a cold Saturday morning?"

"Todd invited Delia over, I didn't want to get in the way."

Gordon shrugged, "Okay."

Before Maggie could walk further Janet Allister walked out of the kitchen, with a cooking flipper in one hand. "I thought I heard you Maggie." She said with a big smile on her face.

Maggie smiled, "Hello Mrs. Allister." She said happily.

Janet was waving her flipper, "Don't just stand there, come and eat some of the chocolate chip cookies I made."

Maggie didn't have to hear any more. She grabbed Gordon's hand and pulled him into the kitchen with her. As they were walking, Mrs. Allister yelled, "I don't want you eating in my kitchen, you'll get in the way. Take a plate of them and go into the living room."

"I love your mom's cookies." Maggie said as they reached the kitchen. "They're so much better than the ones I try to make."

Gordon pulled out a plate from the cupboard, "Please, take as many as you want. If I keep eating them I'll get fat." Gordon said with a laugh in his voice.

Maggie shook her head, poking Gordon in the stomach she said, "I doubt that will happen."

He grinned and started putting cookies on a plate. "Do you think six is good?"

Maggie laughed, "Five for me and one for you…okay."

Gordon shook his head, "Yeah," he handed the plate of cookies to Maggie, "take these in there, I'll bring the milk."

Maggie nodded and turned to leave. She walked through an opening which led to the dining room. Turning around the corner she walked through another opening that led to the living room. Matt, who was home for the weekend from college, was sitting on the couch with a remote in his hand. He was flipping through channels, but when he was saw Maggie he turned off the television and put the remote down. Eyeing up the cookies in her hand he smiled and patted the seat next to him. "Hey Maggie, come sit down, and bring those cookies." His welcoming face glowed as he grinned.

Maggie walked over and put the cookies on the table next to the couch. She gave Matt her best smile and told him how happy she was to see him again. Matt replied by giving her a quick squeeze of the shoulders and asking, "How's my favorite brother's girlfriend doing?"

Maggie looked up at him and grinned, leaning closer she whispered, "I'm not your brother's girlfriend." Pulling back she let her grin turn into a smile.

"Well," he said, "you should be."

Maggie lifted her eyebrows, "Why," she challenged, "give me one good reason."

He looked up to see Gordon walking in the room. "Because he likes you."

Maggie looked over at Gordon and shook her head, still talking to Matt she said, "Nope, not good enough."

Matt laughed, "You're too much for me." Getting up he stretched and said, "I've got to go…do…something." He started shaking his head as he walked out of the room.

Maggie smiled after him as he left. Gordon sat down and asked, "What was that all about?"

Maggie shook her head, "Nothing." She said smiling.

Gordon grinned, "You're too much for me too."

Maggie smiled and said in a playfully innocent voice, "It's not my fault, really."

Gordon looked down at Maggie. "I know." Then adding, "How are things going with Todd? Is he filling the 'older brother' position like he is supposeed to?"

Maggie leaned against the back of the couch, "I don't think he'll ever be as good of an older brother as you were."

Gordon corrected her. "I still am."

Maggie ignored his comment and continued, "For the most part he is okay, but…" Maggie remembered something she and Delia had noticed. "…Do you ever notice that when you say certain things to him, he'll drift off? It's kind of like he's remembering something from a long time ago."

Gordon lifted an eyebrow, "When does he do this?" He asked.

"I first noticed it the first day he went to school, when we were walking home. Delia said it happened again at the dance, and when she was on the phone with him."

Gordon thought for a moment, trying to come up with a logical explanation. "I'm sure he's just thinking about your mom. You have to put yourself in his shoes."

Maggie nodded, "I know, it's just really weird."

Gordon didn't say anything. He looked down at the floor, and then out the window. Looking back up at Maggie he changed the subject by asking, "How cold is it outside?"

"It's just really windy, a good fall day."

Gordon looked over at Maggie, a grin on his face, and a sparkle of excitement in his eyes. "A good fall day to play football?" He lifted his eyebrows in anticipation.

The corners of Maggie's lips quickly formed a half circle. "Sure, get your brothers, it will be fun."

Gordon jumped up, then reached out his hand and pulled Maggie up. The two walked down the hall and up the steps. When they reached the top, Gordon turned right, and knocked on one of the doors. Matt's voice was heard, he told whoever was at the door to come in. Gordon opened it slightly and poked his head through. "Get your football, we're going outside."

Matt quickly put down what he was working on and got up. He grabbed his jacket from on his bed, and walked over to the door. By this time Gordon and Maggie had already continued on to the next room on the right, Gordon opened the door, and told Josh about the game. He got ready and shortly after the four headed out to the backyard of the Allister house.

Matt spoke out. "I want Maggie on my team." He walked up next to her and put his arm around her shoulder.

Gordon turned, "So I get stuck with Josh?" He asked sarcastically.

Matt tossed the ball to him, "Yup, and we are so going to whip your butt."

Josh took the ball from Gordon and threw it back to Matt. "You guys score on that side," he said, pointing toward the left side of the yard. "And we'll go that way." He pointed to the right side of the yard.

Maggie spoke up. "Touchdowns are in between the two center trees on each side."

The four nodded, and went in different directions. Matt whispered to Maggie, "Do you think you can block Gordon?" He asked her.

She nodded, knowing from experiences in the past.

"Good, then I'll block Josh and we should be okay." Thinking for a moment he added. "Just remember...catch the ball and run."

Maggie smiled, "Got it."

They headed out to the middle of the yard. Gordon and Josh had the ball first. Gordon threw it to Josh, but Matt intercepted it. He quickly turned and threw it to Maggie, she caught it and ran. She didn't get far before Gordon came up behind her and grabbed her around the waist, making her stop. Not being able to run, Maggie tried to get out of Gordon's grip, but he was too strong. Matt raced Josh over to where Maggie was held captive. Beating Josh in the race, Matt took the ball from Maggie and continued to run in the right direction. Josh, however, quickly caught up to him and tackled him. Causing both of them to roll over on the grass.

Maggie and Gordon broke out laughing from where they were standing.

Another attempt to make a touchdown was made. This was followed by another, and many more after that. By lunchtime that afternoon the score was Matt and Maggie, fourteen, Josh and Gordon, thirteen. Around noon Janet Allister called the four teenagers in. She had made sandwiches for them and had them set up on the table. Mr. Allister came in to join them and the six ate and talked for about an hour.

While they were eating Mrs. Allister asked Maggie, "What's this I hear about your brother?"

Maggie looked up, "I'll bring him over one day so you can meet him." She paused for a moment and then added, "He came over from Paris."

At one thirty Mr. Allister got up and left for work. Mrs. Allister started to clean up, and Josh and Matt went back into their rooms. Matt's final words were, "We still have to finish that game."

Maggie suggested that they go back to her house and find Todd, but Gordon said he needed to tell her something. The two of them went up into his room and sat down on his bed.

Gordon turned to face Maggie, he looked deeply into her eyes. "Maggie..." he hesitated, "you know how my dad has been looking for colleges for me?" Maggie nodded and waited for him to continue, but he didn't.

She tried to make sense of what he was getting at. "Yeah?" She finally said.

He spoke in a quite voice, "Well, he wanted to keep all of my options open. And because I'm not going to get a good scholarship like Matt did..." he trailed off.

"Gordon, just say it." Maggie demanded.

He paused before finally letting it out. "I'm joining the Air Force."

Chapter 10

That Saturday morning Todd had walked over to Delia's house. She was outside practicing basketball when he arrived. Todd walked up her driveway watching every move she made. When Delia noticed he was there she smiled. Todd attempted to take the ball with his one good arm. With a quick flick of his wrist he managed to have a tight hold on the ball. Todd looked down at the ball, and then back up at Delia, "Want to play?" He asked her competitively.

Delia was starring down at his cast, "What about your cast?" She asked him.

Todd grinned, "If I only have one arm the game will be fair."

Delia knew he wasn't serious, so she decided to play along. "You don't think I'm any good?" She challenged him.

He tossed the ball back to her, "Let's find out."

The game had begun.

Delia started to dribble the ball, avoiding any contact with Todd. He got into position so he was facing her. Todd stuck out his good arm and tried to intercept her dribbling, this was unsuccessful. Delia quickly moved to the side and turned around, putting the ball up for the shot. It bounced off the rim and went through the net. Delia jumped up in victory. Todd retrieved the ball and attempted to dribble around Delia who had already managed to block him. Delia, with the advantage of an extra arm, easily took the ball back from Todd. She didn't have the ball for too long. Todd reached his arm over to where Delia was dribbling and knocked the ball out of her hands. It bounced down the driveway. Todd ran after it, managing to pick it up. He threw a long shot and tried to make a basket. It hit the backboard and bounced onto the ground. Delia broke out laughing. "Nice shot."

She yelled in between her giggles.

Todd walked up to her, smiling. "I guess I'm not that good after all." He spoke in a quiet voice.

Delia was surprised at the softness of his voice. *He's different from every guy I've ever known*, she told herself. For a moment she stood there thinking about how different Todd was from other people. When she finally realized his constant stare she looked up at him and spoke. "As soon as you get that cast off we'll have a rematch."

He nodded in agreement. "Okay." Todd was quiet for a long time. He couldn't decide if he wanted to tell Delia about his memories of Maggie or not. Something inside of him told him that she would understand when he told her, but another part said that she would tell people and blurt his hurting secret to everyone. He closed his eyes, remembering parts from every scene that played over in his head all day long. Most of them were when his mother would yell at Maggie, and tell her she was useless. Others were when their mother physically abused Maggie. Todd hated remembering those ones, but ever since he had moved back to America they had played over in his mind more frequently.

Delia noticed something was wrong with Todd. She looked at him oddly for a moment, but his eyes were closed and there was a look of hurt on his face. Finally, when she couldn't take the suspense she asked him, "Todd, is something wrong?"

Todd's eyes shot open, he realized that he had been standing there for a long time. He looked intently into Delia's eyes. "If I tell you something, will you please not tell Maggie or Gordon?" He asked her, a desperate look in his eyes.

She nodded slowly, having no idea what she was getting into.

Todd grabbed Delia's wrist and led her over to her front porch. The two of them sat down on the front steps. Todd turned and faced her, this time his face was serious. "Does Maggie ever talk about her mom?" He asked her.

Delia shook her head, "She always told us that her mom died years ago."

Todd looked down, almost as if he was disappointed. "Do you

think she can remember that far back?"

Delia shook her head again, "You'd have to ask her." She paused for a moment, a curious look on her face. "Todd, what's this all about?"

He looked up, his gaze fell upon Delia's eyes, "I don't know if Maggie can remember this, but I can…I can remember it like it was yesterday." He was silent again.

"Remember what?" Delia questioned.

"My mom…and Maggie…and this is really going to sound weird." He shook his head, and starred at the ground.

Delia grabbed onto Todd's good hand, this caused him too look up. "I don't care if it sounds weird." She started, talking with a deep concern in her voice. "Something is eating you up, tell me what it is."

Todd pulled his hand away and started to rub his bad thumb with his good hand. Still staring at his cast he spoke. "The whole reason my parents ever got a divorce was because of Maggie." He paused, trying to order his words correctly. "I don't know if she knows this but, before they split up, when Maggie and I were around four and five, my mom would constantly yell at Maggie. She would say horrible things and would tell Maggie she hated her. My father would always walk in and start yelling at my mom. At this point I would take Maggie upstairs and try to stop her from crying." He stopped, unable to continue talking.

Delia was shocked at what she was hearing, *all these years and Maggie really has been hiding something*, she thought to herself.

Todd continued, "I don't know why she hated her, but she did." He looked directly into her eyes. "My mom would actually hit Maggie, I wouldn't be surprised if Maggie has scars from some of the times my mom had hit her."

Delia finally spoke, "Is that what's been bothering you?" she asked in a quiet voice.

He nodded, "When I was in France I would have dreams remembering every detail of when these things happened. But ever since I came over here I've been remembering them any time someone would say something about Maggie. They've been driving me crazy, I just want them to go away."

Delia had never seen a guy pour his heart out like Todd was doing now. She worried that maybe what he was talking about was worse than he was describing it to be. She had never dealt with anything like this before, and she didn't know what to say. It made her wonder about Maggie, did she know all this or could only Todd remember it. She looked at Todd, there was a plea for help in his eyes. "I don't know what to say." She confessed, "I've never dealt with anything like this before...sorry I can't help."

His expression changed from a helpless, hurting little boy to an understanding seventeen-year-old. "That's okay." He told her, "I guess I just wanted to tell someone. I hope I didn't ruin your day or anything." He stood up and offered his hand to held Delia up. She accepted it and stood up next to him.

"Let's go do something fun." She told him. The two walked down to the end of Delia's driveway and turned onto the street.

Todd looked around at his new room, the walls were a dark shade of red, and there was a fluffy white rug on the floor. All of his things from his room in France had been sent to him, and he had set everything up the way he had it back in France.

Todd liked to keep his room simple. He wasn't the type to have a lot of posters on his walls. The one he did have he had brought over with him and it was all written in French. He had hung that above his bed to remind him of his house back in France.

Todd got up from his desk and walked over to his bed. He fell down on it, closing his eyes and picturing his old house. *My mom always had flowers everywhere...I hated the dumb things.* Todd recalled. Now that he thought about it, the flowers had been a sign of assurance, if there weren't any flowers around, he knew something was wrong.

Todd thought about the large stone house that use to be all his. He used to rule over that kingdom, his mom had never cared, she just told him to keep things under control, and then she would leave. Sometimes not coming back for weeks at a time. The only person that was ever around was Geames, he did everything around the house. You could call him the butler, or you could call him the cook, it didn't matter, Geames did everything.

The house itself was made completely of stone, and looked like a castle. It had a grand stairway of thirty steps to get up to the front door. There was a short stone fence that went from the top of the steps all the way around the house to meet at the other side of the steps. Below the fence was a lush green hill that went down to the road. The driveway was literally an underground cave. At the bottom of the hill was a short paved driveway that went from the road to a garage door indented in the side of the hill. When the garage door opened you could see a long paved, underground driveway that led slightly uphill. This went into the back of the house, then turned upwards until it reached ground level. The driveway extended until you reached the real garage that held up to four cars.

The inside of the house was a masterpiece in itself. The first floor was almost like a grand ballroom. As soon as you walked in the front door you were greeted by a large open space with a marble floor. On either side of this large space was a series of doors. Each door leading to a different room. One of the doors led to another section of the house where all of the workers lived. Geames was in charge of all the workers, it was his job to make sure everything around the house went smoothly. Across from the front door was another grand stairway. This one, however, branched off into two different stairways halfway up. These two led up to the second floor, and were also made out of marble. The second floor was split in half. One half consisted of bedrooms. The other half was Elise's studio. Inside her studio was everything a designer could ever dream of. There were mannequins of every size. Hundreds of different kinds of fabrics and thousands of sketches filled every niche.

Todd fell asleep dreaming about his old house, and all the adventures he use to have living there.

Maggie was sitting on one of the plush chairs in her room. She closed her eyes and let a growing tear run down her cheek. *How could he do this to me?* She asked herself. *He's never flown a plane in his life, how is he supposed to learn?* Maggie tried to remember the conversation they had after he broke the news.

"What?" Maggie couldn't believe what she had just heard.

"I know it's a lot but-"

Maggie cut Gordon off, "Gordon, you've never flown a plane." She reminded him.

He nodded, "I know, but they teach you."

She paused before saying, "What if you get killed?"

He looked down, "There's not a war going on, I won't get killed." Before she could say anything he added, "I know this is a lot, but you have to look at it from my point of view. If I join the Air Force they'll pay my way though college and give me a life pension. After four years I'll only be in Reserves anyway. It's not that bad Maggie."

Maggie opened her eyes but everything was blurry. She tried to wipe the tears from under her eyes before she drifted into a deep sleep.

Mr. Morgan was sitting at his desk deciding whether or not he should call Samantha again. The last time he called she didn't seem to mind talking to him again. To him it sounded like she was enjoying the conversation, but he would never know for sure.

Slowly picking up his cordless receiver he dialed her number. A child's voice answered the phone. "Hello?" the ten-year-old boy asked.

"Is your mother there?" Jacob asked his son.

The boy not knowing whom it was let the phone drop onto the table and called for his mother. Jacob could hear the conversation they were having thousands of miles away. After a long wait Samantha finally picked up the phone. "Hello." She said, expecting to be speaking to a salesperson.

Jacob softened his voice. "Hello Samantha."

"Jacob," She sounded surprised, "I didn't think you would call again." She explained to him.

He ignored her comment. "I was thinking about you today." He told her, "So I decided to call."

"Oh." She spoke in a soft, nervous voice. After being silent for a long moment, Samantha decided to tell Jacob what she had been thinking for a long time. "Jacob..." she hesitated, "I really miss you." She finally told him.

He had hoped for her to say that. "I really miss you too."

When Maggie and Todd woke up the next morning their father was waiting for them in the kitchen. After both his children sat down he said, "Something has come up," He chose his words carefully, "And I have to take a business trip out of state."

"Where are you going?" Todd asked, interested in the dealings of his father.

Mr. Morgan hesitated, "Nevada."

Maggie drew in a deep breath, as she flared at her father again.

Todd wasn't affected the same way Maggie was. He started to ask more questions. "How long will you be gone?"

"A little more than a week."

Maggie pushed her chair back and stood up. Without saying anything she turned and walked out of the kitchen and towards her study. Todd watched her with a confused look on his face. He turned to his father.

"What wrong with her?" He asked.

"I don't know." Jacob Morgan lied.

Chapter 11

Jacob Morgan left around noon that same day. He had tried to say goodbye to his daughter, but Maggie refused to see him before he left. Maggie watched him pull out of the driveway from the window in her study. As soon as the car started down the road she left her study.

She found Todd flipping through channels on the television in the living room. He looked up and smiled. "You came out," he started, "can I ask why you ever went in?"

Maggie silently walked over to the couch and sat down next to him. "Dad's not going to Nevada for business." She spoke bluntly.

Todd looked confused, "Then why would he go there?"

"Did I ever tell you about what happened when dad and I moved to Nevada?" Maggie questioned him.

Todd shook his head.

Maggie told him the same story she had told Gordon almost a month ago. After she was finished Todd had the same look on his face that Maggie had when she first found out their father was going.

"I can't believe dad would do that." He said as he shook his head. Looking up at Maggie he asked, "So I really have a brother?"

Maggie nodded, "His name is Kevin."

Todd didn't say anything. He stared at Maggie. *How can a girl that has gone through everything she has be so full of life and happy all the time?* He turned to her, "Do you want to go do something?"

Maggie tried to force a smile, "Sure."

Todd was clueless about what they could do. After a moment of thinking he suggested the game of Battleship. Maggie agreed and went to find the game. She met Todd back in the living room where they both sat on the floor, one on each side of a coffee table that was centered in front of the main couch. They spent the first few minutes setting up their game pieces and thinking of how they would encounter their opponent.

Maggie learned early in the game that Todd was a very competitive person, and he laid out a complex plan for everything he did. Todd sank the first ship, but Maggie came back and sank two of his in her next few turns. The game went on for almost an hour. Finally Todd realized he had met his match in Battleship, he surrendered his last ship and suggested they eat some lunch.

They both set about the kitchen looking for something to eat. Maggie quickly found a package of soft pretzels in the freezer. She asked Todd if that would be okay, he agreed and Maggie turned on the oven and put them in. They only took a few minutes to cook, so while they were in the oven Todd heated up some dipping cheese in the microwave. The two of them ate silently at the kitchen table. After a long moment of silence Todd asked, "Maggie, how do you know dad isn't going away on business?" Todd didn't want to believe that their father would lie to them.

Maggie knew the answer immediately. "Because dad has never had business in Nevada, and I usually take care of all his new business transactions, so I would know if he had any new clients."

Todd noticed how professional Maggie started to sound. *She must help dad run his business,* he thought to himself. *There is no way he could do it by himself.* Another question popped into Todd's mind. "How many people in this town work for dad?"

Maggie shrugged, "Definitely more than half." She paused for a moment, "I don't think they work directly under him, but they probably work at the businesses he owns, so in the long run they work for him."

"Dad owns other businesses?" Todd kept questioning.

Maggie nodded, "Dad has some kind of agreement with almost every organization in this town. The one's that decide not to get support from dad usually go out of business, or don't have too much business."

Todd was deep in thought. *I can't believe dad would leave us and not tell us the real reason he is going. I wonder what else dad has done?* The question hung in the back of Todd's mind for the next few days.

The weekend dragged on. Todd and Maggie took turns suggesting things to do. They ended up finding every single board game Maggie had hidden in the house. After playing each one a few times they would add it to the growing stack in the corner of the living room, and go find another one.

On Sunday night Maggie showed Todd how to get up to the attic. They started looking through some of the boxes, seeing what they could find. Maggie was surprised to find about ten boxes full of Todd and Maggie's baby and toddler clothes. They also found three boxes packed full of old picture books. Maggie leaned against the wall and opened one of them. Todd sat down next to her and watched Maggie as she turned the pages, taking in every picture as if it was a piece of history.

The first book was full of Todd and Maggie when they were newborn babies. There were only a few pictures of their parents, but none of them together. Maggie put that picture book down and picked up the next one. It looked older, and the pictures inside proved it to be so. They were all of Jacob and Elise. Maggie didn't recognize where they were taken, but Todd perked up when he saw a fountain in the background of the third picture.

"They are at the *Huit Vert* Garden. It was mom's favorite place...now I think I know why." Todd looked over at Maggie. "Did dad ever talk about mom?"

Maggie shook her head, "He never mentioned her after he got remarried to Samantha."

Todd didn't say anything, he was starring at a picture of Elise and Jacob holding hands while they were sitting on a stone bench. The two looked very happy to be together. "I bet they never knew that in a few years their lives would change forever and it would affect so many people around them."

Maggie looked up at him questioningly. "What do you mean?" She asked him about the second half of his comment.

Todd tried to explain, "Don't you ever wish mom and dad would have stayed together?"

Maggie slowly started to shake her head, "I don't remember what mom was like, but I remember being the only reason mom left. I wouldn't want to live with someone that hated me that much."

Todd instantly regretted asking that. The memories came back to him. *"Don't ask me for a drink!" Maggie's mom screamed, "Get your own drink!" Maggie was carrying a small empty glass and was holding it up to her mother politely asking her for a drink of juice. Todd was sitting at a kitchen chair watching them, knowing that in a few minutes their world would continue its cycle and everyone would start to yell again. "I just want a drink of juice." Maggie said in a quiet voice. Her mother lost it, "Give me that cup!" She yelled. Quickly grabbing the cup from Maggie's small hands she violently opened the fridge door and pulled out a container of grape juice. Pouring some into the cup she shoved the cup back into Maggie's hands, causing some to spill onto the floor. This made Elise even madder. "You stupid child!" She screamed. Maggie's mother pushed Maggie backwards, she tripped and fell over, causing the rest of the juice to spill. Elise looked as if she was going to kill Maggie. Todd was afraid she was going to except Jacob Morgan walked in the room asking what was wrong. He saw his daughter on the floor and knew immediately. Jacob stayed calm. As he helped Maggie up he glared at his wife. Maggie ran to Todd and watched as Jacob confronted his wife and asked her in a low voice what she had done. Todd knew it would be bad for Maggie to hear this so he led her upstairs to her room and pulled out a clean shirt for her to change into.*

Maggie was looking at Todd. She decided not to ask him if he was okay. This time she wanted to watch him as the expressions on his face changed every few moments. He was lost in his trance for more than five minutes, Maggie started to get worried. "Todd are you okay?" She asked her motionless brother.

Immediately his head shot up and he looked at Maggie, realizing what had just happened. "Yeah, I'm fine." He lied. Inside Todd was worried. He was worried that they would find something in all these boxes that wasn't meant to be found. After what happened that morning Todd was sure that their father was hiding something bigger from Maggie. Todd was afraid that Maggie would uncover it and that secret would scar her for life.

Todd remained silent while Maggie continued to turn through the pages of the old picture books. He was trying to keep out of his miscellaneous trances, but still trying to think about their mother when Maggie was little. *What did Maggie ever do to mom?* He kept asking himself.

Maggie put down the third picture book and picked up the next one. This one looked like the oldest out of them all. Maggie opened to the first page and was shocked to see old pictures of when Elise was a young child.

These pictures caught Todd's attention. "She looks just like you." He commented.

It was true. The small girl in the pictures looked like a younger version of Maggie, only with lighter hair. She was wearing a big smile, and had on a yellow summer dress. Todd pointed to the background and told Maggie that the picture was more than likely taken in one of their grandmother's gardens.

As Maggie continued to turn through the pages, Todd went over to a pile of boxes a few feet away. He blew the dust off of the top box and opened it up. Inside was what looked like colorful pieces of cloth. Todd pulled the top one out of the box and was surprised to see that it was a dress. He turned to Maggie and tried to hold it up to himself, using only his good arm.

"What do you think about this?" He asked, pretending to be modeling the dress. Maggie turned to see what he was talking about. She caught her breath as she looked at what Todd was holding up. "It's beautiful!" She gasped. Getting up she walked over to Todd to get a closer look at the dress he was holding. It was a light blue sleeveless, silk dress. There was a low dip in the front and a fitted waist. The bottom of the dress hung straight down, but it had a wave to it that gave the dress some form.

"You should go try it on." Todd suggested as he watched Maggie look over the dress with wide eyes.

Maggie thought about it for a moment, but then decided against it. "I will later." She told him. Maggie set the dress down and picked up the next one in the box. This one was made of silk as well, only it was light purple. It was long and thin, and had a straight, cut off top. There were sleeves, but no shoulder, and the sleeves went down to right above the hand. On the front of the dress was a sparkling, silver design. It was a twisted and turning line that went all the way down the front.

Maggie was about to pick up the next one when Todd pulled out a series of papers and caught her attention. She moved over to where she could see what they were. The first few pages were an assortment of dress designs. All colored and labeled. On a few of them were side notes that were written in red pen, explaining the dress or saying something about it. Todd was about to put them back in the box when he came across a letter. It was addressed to Elise and written in French.

Elise,

J'ai examiné vos conceptions de robe et je suis très impressionné avec votre travail. Il y a une grande attende d'offre de travail ici pour vous. Vous seriez séance la droite á côté de me sur les trônes du monde de conception. Je sais que cela il n'y a pas persuader vous de faire n'importe quoi vous ne voules pas faire, mais vous souvernir de je suis toujours ici ou' jai toujours été. Je ne comprendrai jamais pourquoi que vous avez choisi d'épouser ce gars de Morgan, mais je suis toujours ici si vous jamais voules me revenir.

J'ai entendu de votre mere que vous avez maintenant deux enflants. Jumeaux. Comment exciter. Un jour je devrai les rencontrer. Est-ce qu'ils sont aussi beau que vous êtes?

J'espere que vous et moi utilise pour avoir. Il simplement devrait

vous rappelez que je vous et moi attends ne vous oubliera jamais.
Amier toujours,
Piere Meiblurle

Todd's face turned white. He silently read the letter through again. Making sure he took in every word. Maggie stared at the letter, not knowing what it said, or why it was making Todd look like he had seen a ghost.

"What does it say?" Maggie finally asked, unable to take the suspense any longer.

Todd slowly translated the letter into English. "Elise, I have looked over your dress designs and I am very impressed with your work. There is a great job offer waiting here for you. You would be sitting right next to me on the thrones of the design world. I know that there is no persuading you to do anything you don't want to do, but remember that I am always here where I have always been. I will never understand why you chose to marry that Morgan guy, but I am always here if you ever want to come back to me. I have heard from your mother that you now have two children. Twins. How exciting. Someday I will have to meet them. Are they as beautiful as you are? I hope you understand that my reason for writing is not to bring you back to the life you and I use to have. It is merely to remind you that I am waiting for you and I will never forget you. Love Always, Piere Meiblurle."

Maggie tried to comprehend the letter, "What does it mean?" She asked Todd.

Todd started to yell. He wasn't yelling at Maggie, he was yelling out of the anger he had for his mother. "It means that all those times mom went on week long business trips she was going to see this guy! It means that the reason she never cared what I did, or whom I was with, was because her thoughts were wrapped around what she would be doing with this guy that night! It means that the only reason mom ever wanted to divorce dad was because she was having an affair!" Todd suddenly realized that he was yelling. Slowly he lowered himself down, leaning against the wall he starred at the letter again.

This time in a calmer voice he said, "I just don't get why our parents couldn't be normal. Why couldn't they just love each other and make our lives easier?" Todd looked over at Maggie, who had sat down next to him, for an answer.

Maggie didn't know what to say to him. She didn't know what was going on in his mind, but she felt bad for him and wanted to cheer him up somehow. "I don't know." Was all she could say, "I guess it's just something we have to live with."

He looked down at his cast, "I don't want to live with it."

"There's not much you can do about it now." Maggie hoped he would just forget about it and they could get on with their day.

Todd was silent, he was thinking about the night of the accident. They were driving home from Elise's biggest fashion show. Todd would have stayed home except his mother told him that they had hired a group of girls his age as models. Todd decided to go and check it out. As it turned out, there were seven girls only a year younger than he that doted on him all night. He had a great night, and couldn't wait for the next day when he had promised one of them they would get together.

The car was about to turn onto Todd's street when a truck, that was too big to fit down the small lanes of the street, ran headfirst into the car Todd and his mother were in. Todd's arm hit the side door at such a force that it cracked in half, and the bone had punctured a small portion of the skin just under his elbow. Todd had gripped his arm in pain and turned to see his mother who was lying unconscious over the dented steering wheel. Her head had a large cut in it, and there were small cuts from the broken windshield. A few minutes later they were carefully taken out of the car and put into separate ambulances. The next thing Todd could remember was laying in a hospital bed with a cast that went over his elbow. It was around one o'clock that morning, but there seemed to be something important going on in the room next to him. A few minutes later he overheard someone in the hallway say the woman from the car accident was nearing death and there wasn't anything they could do to stop the bleeding.

Chapter 12

Maggie and Todd went back downstairs after seeing the letter. They continued in their own way for the remainder of the day.

The next morning they got themselves ready for school and continued their day as if nothing had happened over the weekend. Maggie tried to act as normal as she could, but she found herself drifting off and separating herself from the majority of the people around her. Throughout the day various people asked her if she was okay. Maggie would merely answer that everything was fine and she was just a little tired.

Todd on the other hand tried to be more talkative and did not have any time to think about what he had learned the day before. He tried to be the Todd Morgan that he was before he came over from Paris. He tried to be the charming, but not too sensitive guy he was a few weeks ago. In a matter of a few periods, Todd became the talk of the school once again. This time, however, it wasn't because he was the new kid. It was because Todd was starting to fulfill his role as a Morgan, and other people were starting to notice.

Todd was walking back from French with Kailey when she asked him, "Will you help me study for the French test tomorrow?"

He looked down at her and nodded, "When?"

She smiled at him, "Whenever you want." Kailey let her flirtatious side take over.

"How about after school?"

She nodded and told him they could meet in the library. Kailey turned around the corner and went her separate way.

Todd continued walking until he reached the end of the hallway. He was about to turn the corner when Delia bumped into him, dropping her books onto his feet. She let out a quiet, short scream. Todd grinned and bent down to pick up her books. When Delia finally realized whom she had bumped into, she spoke.

"I'm sor…" Delia tried to apologize, but was silenced by Todd's growing smile. He silently handed back her books and watched her as she turned to leave. Todd stared after her as she walked away. After Delia had turned the corner, Todd continued on his way to Social Studies.

Delia met Todd in the cafeteria. The two sat down at their usual table and waited for others to join them. Todd asked Delia how her weekend had gone.

She smiled, "It was okay…how was yours?"

A mischievous look appeared on Todd's face. "Well I had a lot of fun on Saturday," he said, hinting that he had a good time with Delia. "But Sunday wasn't nearly as fun."

Delia's smile grew. "Are you and Maggie doing anything after school today?" She questioned him.

He thought for a moment, "I don't think Maggie is, but I'm staying after to help someone with French."

"Oh…" Delia paused for a moment, "…who?"

Todd hesitated, "Kailey."

"Oh." Delia said again. This time, however, she sounded disappointed.

Todd sensed that Delia felt uncomfortable. "Are you going to get together with Maggie?" He asked, slightly changing the subject.

She nodded, "I think so."

He smiled, "Good…I'll see you when I get home."

Delia hoped he didn't see the way her cheeks started to blush.

Later that day, when Maggie was in Reading, Kailey walked up to her. "Hi Maggie." She exclaimed happily.

Maggie returned her greeting. "How has your day been?" She asked politely.

"It's been okay…I guess." A girlish smile formed on the corners of Kailey's lips.

Maggie laughed, "What?"

"Do you think your brother might like me?" She asked bluntly.

Here we go again. Maggie thought to herself. "I don't know." She lied. "Why?"

"Because I think I like him…and I just wanted to know if he liked me back."

"Todd doesn't tell me those things." Maggie lied again.

"Okay." Kailey said in a perky voice. She turned around and walked over to her seat.

Todd walked into the library and looked around. He had never been in the library before and was actually amazed at the size of it. He noticed Kailey sitting at a round table on the far side of the library. He slowly walked over to her. She was looking down at her paper and didn't see him walk up. As Todd got closer she noticed him. Looking up she smiled. "Hi!" She exclaimed.

He smiled, and sat down in the chair next to her.

She handed him a piece of paper with a few words scribbled on them. "These are the words I have the most trouble with.

He looked over the page, and nodded. Leaning back in the chair he started quizzing her. "Okay…how do you say *furniture*?" He asked.

"No, no, no…you have to give me the French words."

Todd laughed, "That's the cheaters way out." He told her.

She smiled, "Well then, I guess I'm a cheater."

Todd shook his head and tried again. "What does *Chemise* mean?" He asked.

She was silent for a minute. "Chair?"

He shook his head, "No, *chair* is *Chaise*…*Chemise* means shirt."

Kailey sighed, "I'm never going to get this." She mumbled.

Todd tried to encourage her, "Sure you will, it just takes some time."

She was looking at the floor. "Yeah, but I'm not good at this memory thing."

"Maybe you just have to make it interesting." He suggested.

She looked up, curious about what he meant. "What do you mean?" She asked.

"Wouldn't you remember something better if you were having fun while you were doing it?" He asked her.

She slowly nodded. "Yeah, but how do you make French interesting?"

He grinned. "Pretend you're writing a letter to your boyfriend. He lives in France, and he speaks French. You want to tell him about this killer outfit you just bought. How would you say it?" Todd handed her a blank piece of paper and a pencil.

Kailey thought for a long time. "I can't write a whole letter in French." She finally said.

"I'll help you with most of it, you just worry about the words you should already know." Todd leaned forwards so he could see what she was writing. "First you have to put the date." He told her.

Kailey started to write. *Le 18 novembre,* "Is that right?" She asked him.

He nodded, "What do you want to say next?"

"I went to the store and bought a very pretty dress." She told him.

"Okay, what words do you know in that sentence?"

"I know *dress*, and *store*."

"Okay, so write *durer le mardi je suis allé au,* and write the word for *store*."

Kailey did what he said.

"Now write *et ai acheté une très jolie,* and put the word for dress."

Todd and Kailey worked on the letter for twenty minutes. Finally, when Kailey finished it she leaned back and exclaimed, "That was hard."

Todd laughed, "It wasn't that hard." He told her.

Todd continued to quiz Kailey on the vocabulary words for another half an hour. Around three-thirty, he looked up at the clock on the wall and told Kailey he should be going. Todd helped her pack up her things and put them all into her backpack. He walked her out of the building and said goodbye as he turned the opposite way to start walking home.

When Todd got back to his house Maggie and Delia were in Maggie's study talking. Todd interrupted their conversation by knocking on the door. Maggie ended her conversation and told him he could come in. Todd sat down on the couch next to Delia, and asked them what they had done all day.

"Nothing nearly as exciting as you were." Delia teased him.

Todd leaned back on the couch, "Why do you persist in making my life miserable?" He asked in a jocular tone.

Delia laughed, "Because it's fun and really easy." She told him. A smile spread across Delia's face.

Maggie watched from her chair and smiled, *they are so cute together.* She told herself. As she was watching them, Maggie suddenly wished Gordon were there. *He can't be here all the time.* The protective voice in her head told her. *If he is always here, you won't be special to him anymore.* Maggie didn't believe what the voice inside of her was saying, but she did know that Gordon couldn't always be around her and she was foolish to think that he could. *I wonder what he is doing now?* She asked herself. Maggie knew the answer. He was probably sitting in his room doing homework at his desk. There was more than likely some kind of snack right at his fingertips. Gordon always eats while he works.

Delia had completely forgotten Maggie was in the room. "When do you think you will get your cast off?" She asked Todd hopefully.

"I'm going in over the weekend to have it looked at." He told her, "But I don't think it's healed yet…it's only been about four weeks."

"How bad was is hurt?"

"I don't know…they drugged me up and I don't remember any of it. But I do know that the bone was completely cracked, and it punctured my skin some. So it's probably really bad."

Delia cringed, "Owe." She mumbled.

Todd grinned, "I try not to think about that night." He said quietly.

Delia tried to smile, "Sorry." She apologized.

He shook his head, "It's not your fault."

She was silent while she questioned herself on what she should say next. "Did you have fun with Kailey?" She asked curiously.

Todd looked down, slightly embarrassed, "I don't know...I would rather have been here." He said cleverly.

Delia looked over at him. She was biting her bottom lip, hoping again that Todd couldn't see the burning redness on her cheeks.

Chapter 13

Mr. Morgan came home the next Saturday. By the time he got home, Maggie was ready to forgive him. She met him at the door and told him she was sorry for getting mad. He accepted her apology by embracing her and giving her a fatherly kiss on the forehead. Todd stood in the background and waited for Maggie to finish. When she was done he walked up to his father and welcomed him back. Mr. Morgan smiled down on his son. Finally he said, "I never told you how much I love having my son back. And I feel bad for not telling you until now."

Todd told him that it was okay and he understood. Jacob was about to settle in when he looked down at his watch. He turned to Todd and said, "We're going to be late for your appointment."

Todd laughed, "That's okay..." slipping his shoes on he added, "lets go."

Todd and Jacob got in the car, right before they were about to leave Maggie came running out of the house. "I want to come!" She screamed as she opened the back door of the car and hopped in. Todd looked back at her and smiled, "Buckle up." He told her as they drove away.

She pushed her blown hair back into its place. Reaching for her buckle, she snapped it in place and leaned back. Maggie was silent for the whole ride. She was looking out the window watching the houses go by. She listened to her father and Todd talk about what had happened all week. Her father finally admitted that he had gone to visit his former wife. Todd didn't say anything, he merely nodded. Maggie listened to her father, trying not to get mad at him. She didn't hate him for what he had done. After reading the letter sent to her mother from all those years ago, Maggie had a new perspective on some of the things her father did. She felt bad for him because his wife left him. She also felt bad because he let his work get in the way of another relationship that might have worked.

Maggie was still in deep thought when they pulled into the parking lot of Maggie's doctor. Todd was going to register there as a new patient, and have the doctor look at his arm and see what they could do.

The office was very impressive. It had all the facilities of a hospital, only it wasn't as big with that many beds. The technology was up to date, with all the latest developments in the medical field. Todd was impressed when he walked in at the size of the waiting room. Jacob Morgan walked up to the front desk and was greeted by the young receptionist. Jacob explained to her about Todd, and said they should already have an appointment made for him. She checked her computer and nodded as she handed him the insurance form. Jacob Morgan politely sat down and started to fill it out. Asking Todd about all the questions.

"When did you have the chickenpox?" He asked his son.

Todd shrugged, "When I was six or seven."

He watched as Mr. Morgan made up a date. "What about immunization shots? Have you had any?"

Todd shook his head, "It's not necessary over there."

Mr. Morgan shook his head, "You're going to have to get them. If they find out that I'm sending you to school without them we might have to face a law suit."

Todd laughed at his father, "I thought you had some power in this town?" he asked.

Jacob smiled, "I do…but we would be dealing with the State Health Department, and they don't like me."

Maggie started to laugh. "We'll never forget that one, will we?"

Jacob and Maggie started to laugh at an inside joke. Todd figured it was something that had happened a while ago, and he would find out when someone wanted to tell him.

A few minutes later Todd was called into the room. Mr. Morgan went in with him so he could answer all the questions that were asked. Maggie silently followed behind so she wouldn't be sitting alone in the waiting room. There were four of them in the room Todd was assigned to. The doctor was looking at the records that had been sent over from France.

"A car accident." He said to himself. Turning to Todd he said, "From the looks of it, that bone is very broken."

Todd nodded.

"I want to get a good look at it." He motioned for Todd to follow him to the x-ray room, where they could get a good look at the bone.

Maggie and Mr. Morgan stayed in the room. While they were there Maggie asked, "Did you have fun visiting Samantha?"

Her father was quiet for a long moment. Finally he spoke, "Maggie, I want you to understand something." His voice now had a deep fatherly ring to it.

Maggie waited for him to continue.

"I know you were never fond of Samantha, but you really never gave her a chance."

Maggie didn't say anything, there was a small tear forming in the corner of her eye.

"You have to understand…that night your mother left, it wasn't because of you, it was because she was in love with someone else. That person was my best friend for the few years that I lived in France, and it really hurt me that she would leave me for him." He paused for a moment.

Maggie realized that this was probably very hard for him to tell her these things. "When we moved to Nevada and I met Samantha…well…she listened to the things I said, and she understood what I was going through." He paused once again, "I don't want you to hate Sam. She's a really good person, and she said that she would love to meet you again." Jacob looked at his daughter, hoping she would understand some of the things he was trying to tell her.

Maggie let the tear slowly run down her face, "Daddy…" Maggie took a deep breath an said, "I've never had a mother…the one I did have left me. When I saw you and Samantha together I was afraid I would lose you too." Maggie started to cry. "I didn't want to lose you." She said between the tears.

Jacob walked over to Maggie. He held out his arms and welcomed her into his embrace. "I'll never leave you." He told his daughter. "You mean the world to me." Maggie leaned her head against her father's chest. Mr. Morgan held onto his daughter, "I love you." He told her. "I love you."

The doctor and Todd came back into the room a few minutes later. Mr. Morgan and Maggie continued to talk. Mostly about the things from Mr. Morgan's past. The doctor said that Todd's arm was healing extremely fast and he would be able to get rid of the cast in two weeks.

"In the mean time." The doctor continued, "I want to take this cast off and give him a smaller one. That way the wound on the skin can heal also." Mr. Morgan nodded in agreement.

The doctor went into a small cabinet and pulled out some supplies. Maggie watched in amazement as he dug what looked like a small blade into the cast. Todd sat there calmly. He was use to the procedure of getting a cast taken off.

The doctor worked his way down the cast with the small blade. The doctor was telling Mr. Morgan how this new kind of blade isn't able to cut anything that isn't cast material. Maggie noticed how the doctor was especially careful around the spot Todd had said the puncture in his skin was. The doctor peeled away the cast and exposed Todd's weak arm. Maggie looked at the huge bruise at the top of his forearm, right below the elbow. It had a small red mark in the middle, where the bone had almost punctured though the skin.

As the doctor prepared the new cast, Todd picked his arm up with his good arm and tried to move it. He slowly bent it, still supporting it with his other arm. The doctor turned his attention back to Todd. First he wrapped a layer of padding around Todd's arm. Next he wrapped a roll of wet padding around Todd's arm. The wet padding was mixed with plaster and hardened after a few minutes.

Todd's new cast didn't go over his elbow. This way he didn't need a sling and he could bend his elbow. The doctor said it would also allow the wound on the skin to heal faster. Todd thanked the doctor and the three Morgans left the room. Mr. Morgan made an appointment for Todd to go back in two weeks, and they left.

On the way back to the house, Mr. Morgan asked Maggie, "What did you do all week?"

She shrugged, "Not much…I did a lot of thinking."

Mr. Morgan nodded, "Me too." Then he added to both his children, "I'm very proud of both of you."

Todd looked over at him. "Why?" He questioned.

Mr. Morgan shrugged, "I just am."

When they got back to the house Mr. Morgan said he had to get some work done. He apologized to his children and promised them he would make it up to them. Todd escaped and went to visit Delia. Maggie stayed home for another half an hour. Finally the phone rang. She answered it and was surprised to hear Gordon on the other end.

"Hi." Gordon said, he sounded like he had been in deep thought about something for a long time.

"Hi." Maggie returned his greeting.

"Are you busy today?" He asked.

Maggie told him she wasn't.

"Would it be okay if I came and visited you?" He asked.

For a minute Maggie thought he was nervous. "Yeah."

"Good." Gordon replied. "I'll see you in a few minutes."

Maggie hung up and leaned back in her chair, waiting.

Gordon arrived a few minutes later. He pulled up in his car and slowly walked up to the front door. Maggie opened it and met him on the porch. She smiled, "Hi."

He smiled back, but didn't say anything. He stood in silence for a few minutes before speaking. "Look Maggie-"

She cut him off. "It's okay." She said in a quiet voice.

He ignored her and finished, "Maggie, this past week was the worst week of my life. Even though we talked some and I still saw you, I felt like I'd lost you. I don't want to lose you ever again."

Maggie smiled, but didn't say anything. She stepped forward and welcomed Gordon into a hug. She leaned her head against his chest and took a deep breath. *He's back.*

Chapter 14

The two weeks passed quickly, and when it was time for Todd to get his cast off he was more than ready. Mr. Morgan drove both of his children to the doctor's office. He and Maggie waited patiently in the waiting room while Todd went in with the doctor to have his cast removed.

While he was in there, Mr. Morgan asked his daughter, "Maggie, what do you think about going to visit Samantha?"

Maggie looked at her father in shock. "What do you mean?" She asked him.

He was silent for a moment. "I guess I shouldn't say visiting." He was very hesitant, "What I'm trying to say is, Samantha and I have been talking and we have decided to get back together."

Maggie didn't realize what he was getting at. She merely nodded and waited for him to continue.

Jacob looked at his daughter seriously, "Maggie…Samantha and I have been discussing it, and we feel that it would be better if we moved to Nevada instead of her moving here."

Maggie didn't say anything. Slowly all of the color left her face. She starred at her father blankly. "Wha…?" She tried to ask him.

"I know it's hard to take in…but I really think it will work out." He tried to explain. "They have a great school and there are a lot of people around. You and Todd will do fine."

Maggie shook her head, she was trying not to get mad at her father. "I don't want to leave dad. I want to stay here…with the friends I already have. I want to stay at my school…and at my house."

"I'm sorry Maggie. I know I should have talked it over with you, but you have to try to understand." He tried to apologize to Maggie.

Maggie looked down at her feet. "What about Todd, did you tell him yet?" She asked.

He shook his head, "I was going to talk to both of you when we got home...but I thought I would tell you now."

Maggie was quiet again. Finally she looked up at her father and said, "I don't want to move daddy." A small tear ran down her cheek.

Instantly Mr. Morgan felt bad. "I know you don't want to...but it's just something to try for a while."

"When are we going?" She questioned.

"Next week."

Todd was about to head out the door when his father stopped him.

"Where are you going?" Mr. Morgan asked his son.

Todd turned to his father, "I was going to go to Delia's house."

Mr. Morgan nodded, "Can it wait about a half an hour? I have something I want to talk to you and Maggie about."

"Sure." Todd turned around and followed his dad into his study.

Maggie was already sitting at one of the chairs. Her eyes where zoned out, and her face was still colorless. Todd sat down in the chair next to her. Maggie tried to force a smile when he sat down.

Jacob sat down at his desk and turned to face his children. He looked directly at Todd. "I don't know how to say this Todd...but I've decided that we will be moving to Nevada."

A confused look made its way to Todd's eyes. "What?"

"I know it is short notice, but my former wife and myself have come to the decision that we are going to be getting back together. We also decided that it would be for the better if I move in with her."

Todd didn't say anything, he was looking over at Maggie, watching the expression on her face. He closed his eyes and started to remember again.

Maggie was about to walk into her bedroom, but she stopped when she saw the figures of her mother and Todd standing in front of Todd's dresser. Elise sensed the presence of someone else in the room and turned around. She glared down at Maggie, looking her straight in the eye and asking her, "What do you want." Maggie didn't say anything. She just stood in fear and waited for her mother to say something. Elise walked up to Maggie, "Answer me when I talk young lady!" She yelled. Todd feared that his mother would hit Maggie, so he walked over and stood next to Maggie. He looked up at his mother. "Mommy, why don't you like Maggie." His small, innocent voice asked. Elise looked down at Todd and said, "Todd, you are too young to be bothered with such things." She gently pushed him aside. Turning her attention back towards Maggie, Elise continued to glare down at her daughter. Finally Maggie asked, "What are you doing with Todd's clothes?" A sly smile formed on Elise's lips as she answered, "I'm taking Todd and moving, that way we can get away from you."

Todd shook his head, and opened his eyes. He looked up at Maggie, her expression hadn't changed. He turned to face his father. "When are we going?" Todd asked.

"Next Saturday."

"What about the house?" Maggie finally spoke for the first time since Todd had entered the room.

Jacob thought for a moment. "We're going to leave enough stuff in it so you can come back to visit any time."

"Oh." Maggie's expression softened. "Daddy…can I be excused?" She asked him.

He reluctantly nodded, looking after her as she walked out of the room.

Maggie stood on Gordon's doorstep, and waited for someone to answer her knock. A few seconds later Gordon opened the door and let Maggie in, he was about to greet her with a smile when he noticed something was wrong.

A worried expression spread across his face, "What?" He asked, expecting the worst.

Maggie looked down at the floor, in a quiet voice she said, "Samantha and my dad are getting back together…we're moving to

Nevada at the end of the week."

The words hit Gordon like a bullet hitting its target. He closed his eyes to cover the pain that was now showing in them. After a few moments he opened them and looked down at Maggie. She was watching him, taking in every detail on his face. Her eyes had small pools of water under them as she tried to hold in her tears. He tried to smile as he stepped forward and invited Maggie into a hug. She accepted and allowed Gordon to wrap his arms around her waist. Maggie leaned her head on his chest and allowed a tear to run down her cheek.

"You can't leave." He finally said, holding in his pain.

Maggie didn't reply.

Gordon stepped back and looked down at Maggie again. "I don't want you to leave me."

"I have to." Maggie explained to him.

"Why?" Gordon questioned. "Why can't things stay how they are?"

Maggie started to walk towards the door to the living room. Gordon followed her. "I don't know." She told him as she walked. Turning to Gordon she said, "I don't want to make this harder than it really is...I just want to get it over with."

Gordon walked over and sat next to her on the couch. He turned to face her and asked, "Get what over with?"

Maggie looked down, slightly embarrassed about what she was going to say. "Saying goodbye to you." She finally said. "What if I never see you again?"

Gordon reached his hand over and put it on top of Maggie's. "Why wouldn't you?"

"Because you're going away at the end of the year, and I'll be in Nevada."

Gordon suddenly remembered. Hoping Maggie wouldn't see through him he answered, "Don't worry, I'll find a way."

Chapter 15

Gordon silently walked up to Maggie and took her books from her. He didn't say anything, he merely looked at her and smiled. She smiled back and walked silently next to him until they reached Maggie's next class. She finally turned to him and said, "You don't have to go out of your way for me."

His expression didn't change, "I want to spend every moment with you."

Maggie looked into Gordon's eyes. It was the start of eighth period, and Maggie's last day of school at River Valley High was coming to an end. She was leaving first thing tomorrow morning. Gordon said he and Delia were going to the airport before they left. Delia had told Maggie that she wanted to be the last person to hug her goodbye. Maggie had told Delia that would be okay as long as she didn't make her cry.

Gordon handed Maggie's books back to her. She took them and started to turn into her classroom. She was about to enter the doorway when she turned back and looked at Gordon again. His face had a pained expression on it, and for a moment Maggie thought he might cry.

Someone called Maggie's name from inside the classroom, and she turned her head to see who it was. After looking back one more time, Maggie walked the rest of the way into the classroom, leaving Gordon standing alone in the hall staring after her.

Jacob Morgan woke his children up early on Saturday morning. They had less than an hour to get cleaned up and ready to leave. The house was still very full, only the important things were packed up and already on their way to Nevada. Most of their possessions, however, were going to be left at the house for when Maggie and Todd wanted to visit.

Maggie reluctantly got out of bed. She quickly took a shower and did her hair. After packing some final things into her carry on, Maggie took the bag and walked downstairs. She met her father in the den, he was checking things over to make sure they had everything they needed.

Jacob looked up and smiled at his daughter. After saying good morning he asked if Todd was out of the shower yet. Maggie shrugged and kept on walking. She was about to pass her father when he reached out and grabbed her wrist, causing her to turn around in shock.

"I don't want you to hate me." He said in a stern, demanding voice.

Maggie hesitated, "I don't" she lied.

He released his grip from Maggie's wrist and let her walk the rest of the way to the kitchen. She went to the cupboard and pulled out a box of cereal and a bowl. After pouring some cereal into the bowl, Maggie filled it with milk and sat down.

Todd came down a few minutes later. He looked all cleaned up and ready to go. Smiling at Maggie, he got a bowl of cereal for himself and sat down across from her. After a few minutes of silence he asked, "You really don't want to move do you?"

She shook her head, "I've always hated moving."

He thought for a moment, "I've really only moved twice in my life, so things like this are still exciting to me."

"Aren't you going to miss your friends?"

"Which friends?" Todd challenged. He had to admit that after living here for a few months he had only met a small number of people who he could actually consider his friends.

Maggie shrugged, "What about Delia?"

Todd thought about it for a long time. Back in France Todd would have immediately said that he wouldn't miss Delia. But the more he thought about it, the more Todd finally realized that ever since he came to America he had changed. He would usually get over any girl as soon as another one showed an interest in him. But after going through everything that he had, Todd suddenly cared more about a quality friendship than he did about how many girls he could go out with in a week.

He reluctantly nodded.

For the first time that morning Maggie smiled. "I'm glad...now I'm not in this alone."

At eight thirty that morning the three Morgan's packed up and left for the airport. After going through security, they checked in on their flight and sat down in the waiting area. Gordon and Delia arrived a few minutes later. Delia, trying to break the tension of the moment, started complaining about all the security.

Maggie laughed at her friend, "Give it up Deal." She finally said, partially annoyed with all of Delia's yammering.

Delia smiled back. "I love you too." She allowed her lips to curl up into an even bigger smile.

Maggie's face did the same. A few moments later Todd joined in on their conversation. Maggie glanced over at Gordon and noticed him talking to her father. She wondered what they were talking about, but she didn't ask. Turning her attention back to Todd and Delia.

"Now you'll never be able to save me." Delia was saying with a twist in her voice.

Todd grinned. "Yes I will, it will just take a little more planning than I thought." His grin grew. Delia let a big smile make its way onto her face.

The five of them sat down again and waited. A few words were said, but for the most part everyone was quiet. After a few minutes a voice came over the loudspeaker and said that flight 893 to Carison, Nevada, was leaving in five minutes.

The good-byes started.

Delia jumped up, ran to Maggie, pulled her up and hugged her. As Delia looked over Maggie's face she saw an intense sadness. Even when Maggie forced a smile her eyes still showed how sad she really was. Delia tried to imagine what Maggie was going through.

Having messed up parents, just finding out she had a brother, then finding out she had another one, and being forced to leave her friends and go live in another state. Delia couldn't fathom what Maggie was thinking.

After a long goodbye from Delia, the voice came over the loudspeaker again. "All first class passengers and women with children for flight 893 to Carison, Nevada, may now board."

Here we go. Maggie thought to herself as she slowly stood up. She turned to her father. He was watching her. For a moment Maggie thought he might turn back on his decision to leave. But her hopes crashed when he said, "I'm going to board, you two meet me there in a couple of minutes."

Todd and Maggie both nodded. He turned to leave and they turned to face Gordon and Delia. Gordon walked up and shook Todd's hand.

"I guess I'll see you in a couple of months or something." Gordon said as he loosened his grip on Todd's hand.

Todd nodded and walked up to Delia. He looked down at her for a long time, taking in the details of her face. Finally he reached out his arms, and for the first time, Todd hugged Delia. It wasn't a long hug, just long enough for Todd to whisper into Delia's ear that he was going to miss her. When Delia stepped back her face had turned slightly pink, but Todd didn't notice, nor did he care.

Gordon slowly walked over to Maggie. She was staring down at the ground when he walked up to her. Gordon figured she wasn't with it at the moment, and he knew in a few minutes he wouldn't be either. Slowly he reached out his hands and grabbed her elbows. His touch caused her to look up. There were tears growing in her eyes and one already running down her cheek.

Instantly Gordon felt the pain she was feeling. He could feel his throat swell up, and his head starting to think of impossible ways to avoid this. Gordon couldn't say anything, his head started to spin and he couldn't think straight.

Maggie stepped forward and leaned against him. He automatically wrapped his arms the rest of the way around her. Maggie started to cry. "I don't want to go."

Gordon still couldn't say anything. His throat started to throb as he tried to hold back from crying.

Maggie stepped back to look up at him. When she did she saw water welling up at the base of his left eye. Maggie let his arms fall to his side so she could hold onto his hands. He laced his fingers through hers just as the tear in his eye fell down over his cheek.

"Maggie, we have to go." Todd said from behind her.

She started to back up. Gordon tightened his grip on her hands. "Wait." He said in a quiet voice.

Maggie stopped.

Gordon regained his voice. After looking into Maggie's eyes for what seemed like forever, he said, "I love you."

Maggie didn't move. She couldn't. *No…no…* her mind kept telling her that he didn't say that. She looked at him one more time before completely releasing her grip and turning away. She slowly walked towards the boarding door. Gordon watched her hand her ticket to the attendant and continue walking. Right before entering the tunnel, Maggie turned her head and saw Gordon watching her with a growing pain in his eyes. Their eyes met for a brief moment, but Maggie quickly turned around and walked the rest of the way through the tunnel.

Gordon sat back down in his chair and leaned his elbows against his knees. He rested his head in his hands and started to rub his eyes. Delia sat down next to him and gently rested her hand on his shoulder.

"It's okay…they'll be back." She tried to encourage him.

He didn't say anything. After a while, Delia got up and went home. She said goodbye to Gordon, but he still didn't respond. Gordon sat there for another hour before he left.

Chapter 16

Maggie knew which house it was long before they pulled into the driveway. It was the biggest house on the road, and she could still remember it from all those years ago. There was a woman and a young boy standing outside, waiting for them. The woman had long, straight, red hair. She had a tan, which looked like it might be fake, and had on a yellow sundress. The boy was up to her shoulders and she had dark hair like Maggie's father. He had blue eyes, and Maggie thought he might be able to pass for Todd if he didn't have his mother's square face. His hair was shorter on the sides than on the top, and few pieces blew out of place as a slight breeze ran across their faces.

Samantha was smiling, she greeted Jacob with a hug and a kiss. Maggie and Todd lingered in front of the car and took in their new surroundings. It looked like a very residential street. There were a lot of houses and a lot of basketball nets in front of the houses. *Delia would love it here.* Maggie thought to herself.

Samantha's house was a flat-board log cabin. It was a very good-sized house, and had a large front porch. There was a second floor, but it only covered part of the first floor. The roof was black and it fit well with the dark brown house.

Jacob motioned for his children to come join them. Maggie and Todd reluctantly walked up to meet Samantha. She smiled at them and said hello.

"I'm so excited." She told them in a cheery voice. "I can't wait to have a real family again!"

Maggie wanted to say something, but she held back from saying something that she would regret.

Samantha reached her arm over and pulled her son closer to her. Placing her hand on his shoulder she introduced them. "Todd, Maggie, this is Kevin. He's your brother. I hope the three of you get well acquainted."

Todd forced a smile. He and Maggie walked back to the car to get some of their things. As they turned away, Maggie heard Samantha say to Jacob, "I don't think they like me."

Jacob didn't reply.

Maggie felt like she was going to cry. The long hours on the plane hadn't helped the emptiness she felt inside, and she had a feeling that it was only going to get worse. Maggie and Todd took their small bags into the house. They stepped inside and looked around. The other three had already gone in, they were sitting on the couches in the family room, talking and laughing. The house was exactly how Maggie remembered it. The whole first floor had wooden flooring, and light brown trim. The majority of the rooms were painted a light yellow. This reflected the sunlight from the many windows that decorated the walls. As you walked in the front door you were met by a large open space filled with end tables that were decorated with vases of flowers.

On the left side of the room was a staircase. It was wooden with a fluffy off-white rug running down the middle. The stairs were curved, and the staircase ran from the side, around the corner, to the back of the room. They then disappeared into the flooring of the next level. Under the stairs was an entranceway into the kitchen. The kitchen was a medium sized kitchen. It had a dishwasher and double sink. There were light brown, wooden cabinets surrounding the floor and ceiling on two sides. On the third side was a table, and on the fourth side was a fridge, an oven, a stove, and a cutting-board counter. Everything in the kitchen looked unused, just as Maggie remembered it when the house was first built.

Maggie and Todd walked up the steps. At the top of them was a long hallway with two doors on each side. At the end of the hallway was an open space with couches and a huge window that took up the majority of the wall.

Two of the doors were open. They were the farther two and were directly across from each other. Maggie walked forward and was followed by Todd. She turned into one of them. Inside a bedroom was arranged. All of Maggie's and Todd's things had arrived before them, and Samantha had taken the liberty to unpack and arrange their rooms for them. The room Maggie and Todd were standing in appeared to be Todd's. One of his desks was set up on the far wall. On top of it sat his computer and printer. Next to that was his phone. His computer chair was neatly pushed under the desk, waiting to be sat in. A bed sat perpendicular to the desk. It was pushed up against the side wall, with Todd's bedspread neatly tucked into the sides. On the opposite wall was the dresser, on top of the dresser sat Todd's alarm clock and his stereo.

The room was half the size of the one Todd had had at his other house, but he didn't care. He dropped his bag onto the floor and fell onto his bed. Maggie walked over and sat next to him. He looked up at her from where he was lying. "Why aren't you in your room?"

She shrugged and didn't say anything.

Todd lifted his arm and pointed towards his phone. "Call Delia, I want to talk to her."

"Maggie, Gordon's a wreck! I can't believe you left him like that!" Delia screamed over the phone.

Maggie was sitting at Todd's desk, leaning back in his chair. He was watching her from his bed, waiting for his turn to talk. "I didn't know what to say." She said, ending on the wrong note and making the statement sound bad.

"Will you at least call him and talk to him?" Delia begged with her friend.

"Of course…" After a moment, Maggie added, "just not today."

Delia sighed, "You're going to kill this poor boy, and he did nothing to deserve it."

Maggie didn't know what to say. She turned to Todd and motioned for him to leave the room. He did so without question and shut the door behind him. As soon as he left Maggie said, "Now I can talk...my brother is gone."

Delia grinned, "Your brother was there and you didn't let me talk to him?" She asked sarcastically.

"Don't you care about what I'm going to say?" Maggie couldn't help but smile as she waited for Delia's answer.

Letting out another sigh, Delia told Maggie to continue.

"I wanted to say something, but I couldn't. I don't know why...I just couldn't."

"I completely understand...but you left the guy crying for a whole hour before he went home." Delia waited, "You've ruined him."

Maggie felt another tear forming in her eye. "Delia, you just don't get what it's like. Everything inside of me was telling me to just fall into his arms...but when the chance came I knew it would only make things harder than they had to be."

Delia tried to think of something she could say to Maggie. After a long moment of silence she finally spoke, "Look, Maggie, I know you and Gordon have a really special relationship. And I know that you two would never let anything get in the way of that. All you have to do is call him and you will make his year. He loves you, and you'll never find a guy any better than him."

Maggie took in every word Delia said. "Thanks." Maggie's voice had changed into a soft tone. "I really appreciate it." Maggie couldn't help but smile again.

The silence lasted for only a short period. As soon as Delia knew that Maggie was going to be okay she changed her voice and asked, "Can I talk to your bother now?"

Maggie's smile grew, she put her hand over the receiver and yelled Todd's name. He walked in the room a few seconds later. Taking the phone from Maggie, he fell back onto his bed and started to talk to Delia.

Maggie left the room and entered hers. Todd had taken her bag and had put it on her bed. She walked over and opened it. In the front pocket was a tiny stuffed bear. It was brown and was holding a tiny heart. Maggie had had it since last February when Gordon gave it to her on Valentines Day. She took it and placed it on top of her computer. The small bear had a big smile, and Maggie knew she would smile every time she saw it.

Maggie stepped into her first period classroom. She looked around and hated everything she saw. The people were talking amongst themselves, only a few of them noticed the new girl that had stepped into their class. A voice coming from Maggie's left called out her name. For a moment Maggie was motionless. The voice sounded so much like Gordon's she forgot where she was. Maggie turned in expectation, but was disappointed to see a tall boy with dark blond hair. His hair looked like it had some gel in it, but not enough to make it look greasy. He had tanned skin that contrasted to the lightness of his hair. His dark blue eyes sparkled as he smiled at Maggie.

She watched him approach her as he asked, "So you're the girl everyone is talking about?"

Maggie tried not to make eye contact with the attractive guy that stood in front of her. "Everyone is talking about me?" She responded in an unhappy voice.

He raised his eyebrows, "Most girls love it when they are the center of attention."

Maggie looked down at his feet. He was wearing black and grey sneakers with a lime green slash running thought them. "I guess I'm not like most girls then." She said more confidently as she lifted her head to look up at him. This time she allowed herself to make eye contact with him.

His lips slowly began to form the shape of a grin. He broke the silence by saying, "I've heard a lot about you Maggie Morgan." He spoke in a low, ringing voice.

Maggie began to loosen up, smiling she said back to him, "I wish I could say the same."

His grin broke into a smile. "I'm Pete Landers, it's nice to meet you."

Maggie ignored his name, "So what have you heard about me?"

She asked curiously.

Pete thought for a moment, "Only that you're dad is in charge of Morgan Industries, and the WWCC. That right there is pretty impressive."

Ignoring what he said again she asked another question, "So why is everyone talking about me?"

Once again Pete thought for a moment, "Probably because you're new here and you have a world famous father." He noticed that Maggie started to lose interest in what he was saying. She seemed to drift away into her thoughts. "Is there something else on your mind?" He asked, completely changing the sound of his voice.

Maggie was caught off guard again. The tone Pete started talking in sounded like Gordon again. She looked at him with a confused look in her eyes. Shaking her head she lied. "No, I just lost it there for a moment." Maggie turned and walked away, leaving Pete confused about why a girl had lost interest in him.

Todd waited for Maggie outside of her eighth period class. She walked over to him and smiled, "How was your day?" She asked, forcing herself to sound cheerful.

He grinned, "Not near as fun as being the new kid in River Valley. Everyone there knew you, so they automatically liked me. Here I think I might actually have to try to be cool."

Maggie smiled. She was glad to have such a fun brother. She was about to say something when a familiar voice called her name from behind her. She turned around to see Pete walk up to her again. He waved to Todd and smiled at Maggie.

"I was hoping I would catch you before you left." He said as he starred down at Maggie.

She didn't say anything.

"I was wondering if I could show you and your brother around, and introduce you to some of my friends."

Todd was about to accept when Maggie butted in and said that their father would be coming to pick them up and she wanted to go home. Todd told her that their dad wouldn't care and she could go home it she wanted, but he was going to take Pete up on his offer.

Maggie smiled and turned to leave. She found her way out of the building and waited at the curb for Jacob to drive up.

Pete showed Todd the center of the town. It was only a few blocks away from the school, so it was where most of the kids hung out before making their way home. As they walked past a series of small businesses, Pete asked, "Why is your sister so uptight?"

Todd knew the answer right away, but he didn't want to tell Pete too much, "She is taking the whole moving thing pretty hard."

Pete bought what he said and left the question alone. They were silent for a long time until Todd added, "If I were you, I would be careful around her."

Pete gave him a confused look.

"She has her way of influencing peoples' lives. Just be careful that you don't start to like her or anything, with everything that has gone on, it would just be a waste of time." Todd's sentence ended abruptly.

Pete changed the subject and started to talk about all the things there were to do in their small town. Todd paid attention, but his thoughts were elsewhere.

Gordon opened the door to his room and walked in. He threw his backpack off to the side, and flopped down into his chair. He hadn't said much all day, Delia had come up to him once and tried to talk to him, but he didn't respond so she stopped talking. Gordon closed his eyes and fell into a light sleep.

He was awakened by the sound of his mother knocking on his door. She opened it and stuck her arm out. In her hand was the cordless phone. Gordon got up and took it from her. She left the room, closing the door behind her.

"Hello?" Gordon said in a slow, depressed voice.

Maggie couldn't think of anything to say. She wanted to tell him everything, but the only words that came out were, "I'm sorry."

Gordon knew who it was right away. His voice changed and he sounded hopeful. "Maggie?" He asked softly.

"I'm really sorry Gordon."

He sat down on his bed. "You don't have to be…I should be the one apologizing."

Maggie smiled, "So how was your day?" She asked as if she was talking to him from her old house.

"Pretty bad, everyone is still trying to get over the shock of not having you there."

Maggie let her smile fade away.

"So what about you?" He added, "How was your day?"

"Worse than yours."

He grinned, "Did you meet any guys that might be a threat to me?" Gordon tired to cheer Maggie up.

Her smiled slowly came back. "Not really."

"What does that mean?" His grin grew.

She hesitated, "My brother has become best friends with this guy that keeps asking me to do things with him. But I think Todd told him to give it up."

Gordon laughed, "That's good, tell your brother I said thanks."

"Ok."

Gordon changed the subject again, "So what's it like there?"

Chapter 17

Maggie was happy the next day at school. She smiled at everyone, and was starting to get noticed. *I was the new kid once…I can do it again.* The line kept repeating itself inside Maggie's head. During first period Pete came up to talk to Maggie again.

"I'm sorry I pushed you yesterday." His gentle voice caught Maggie by surprise.

She smiled at him, "I'm sorry I was such a grouch."

His lips curved upwards. "It's not your fault…I completely understand being the new kid." He explained just as the bell rang. Maggie smiled and sat down, not saying a word to him for the rest of the period.

Maggie didn't see Pete again until fourth period, during History. When the teacher, Mr. Krunzs, called for partners, Pete stood up and walked over to Maggie. "You look like you need a partner." He grinned.

Maggie looked up at him and smiled back. "I guess I do."

He sat down, turning to face her he said, "I don't want to sound like a dork or anything, but there is something about you that makes me want to get to know you." He paused and tried to explain, "So if I sound a little too anxious sometimes, just bear with me and let it pass."

Maggie didn't know what to say, *This guy is way too much like Gordon*, she told herself, *I've got to back away before I end up losing him too.* A protective voice inside her head kept telling her to be careful and to not be friends with Pete. But another side of her was pushing her towards him, telling her that it was harmless and she shouldn't worry.

Maggie finally nodded, making herself look like a complete idiot. Pete chuckled and then smiled, he turned to face the teacher who had started to explain what they would be doing the next three days.

Back at home things weren't working out as well. Todd and Kevin kept getting in fights. And Jacob always leaned towards Kevin's side of the argument. Maggie would try to defend her brother, but the two of them would always lose. The house was divided. Todd and Maggie barely spoke to anyone except each other. They spent all of their time in either of their rooms, and they ended up doing everything together. They only went downstairs to eat and sometimes to go get something.

Jacob tried to explain to them that Kevin wanted to be a part of their life because he looked up to them. Maggie and Todd just nodded and walked away whenever he brought up the subject.

From her room, Maggie could hear some of the conversations that her father and Samantha had every night. Samantha would complain that she didn't like the way one of the twins was acting, and Jacob would tell her that he would talk to them in the morning.

He is a big book of un-kept promises. Maggie thought to herself one night.

She called Delia once a week, giving her all the details on everything that happened. According to Delia, Todd had been calling her almost every other day, and Delia was enjoying it immensely. Gordon and Maggie didn't talk very often, but when they did, they would talk for hours.

Kailey got up from where she was sitting and ran over to Gordon. Yelling out his name, she caught his attention. He smiled and waited for her to catch up. As soon as she fell into pace with him, he started to talk.

"How have you been?" He asked politely.

She smiled, "Pretty good...you?"

He shrugged, "I'm okay."

Kailey looked up at him, "Do you miss Maggie?" She asked bluntly.

Gordon didn't say anything for a few moments. Finally he looked down at her and nodded.

"You and Maggie were cute together." She continued.

He merely smiled.

She was silent for a moment before adding, "I guess I should get to the point."

Gordon looked down at her.

"A few of my friends and I are worried about you...we think that you have to let Maggie go and be the Gordon we knew before." She had a pleading look in her eyes.

He didn't say anything, so she continued, "We all miss them Gordon, but lots of people have moved away from here and none of them have affected you this way. I've known you my whole life, and I want the old Gordon back."

"Kailey...it's..." He tried to say what he was thinking. "You just don't understand."

"Okay, so maybe I don't, but will you at least hear me out?"

He nodded, she continued, "The Senior Christmas Party is this Friday...I want you to come."

Gordon hesitated before answering, "I...I don't know."

"Yes you do." She insisted, "You've always had fun at these parties, even before Maggie came here...I'm sure you can do it again."

"I'll think about it." With that Gordon turned around the corner, and started his way down a different hall.

Todd opened Maggie's bedroom door and popped his head in. Holding up a phone in his hand he motioned to Maggie that it was for her. She went over to her desk and picked up her phone, placing it next to her ear she said hello.

"Maggie..." The voice sounded like Gordon's.

Happy to be talking to him again, Maggie answered back excitedly,

"Hey Gordon."

The voice was quiet for a moment, "This isn't Gordon...It's Pete."

"Oh!" Maggie exclaimed, embarrassed. "Sorry."

Pete grinned, "That's ok...um..." He hesitated with what he was about to say. "I was wondering if you wanted to get together sometime and do something?"

Maggie was shocked at his question. "Like what?"

"I really don't know." Pete laughed at himself. "We could just get together and do homework or something."

Maggie smiled, "I'd love to."

The two of them met in the library after school the next day. It was empty except for the librarian, who was deeply involved in a thick book. Pete smiled as he sat down next to Maggie. She pulled out her math folder and started to open her book. He followed, after a few moments of silence, Pete broke the ice. "Tell me something about yourself." He said, leaning back in his chair so he was facing Maggie.

A small smile formed on her lips. "What do you want to know?"

He thought for a moment, "Something about your old life."

Maggie closed her eyes. Her mind jumped back to when she first met Gordon. Bending her knees so she could pick up her books, she remembered being at eye level with a guy that was doing the same thing. He handed back her folder and smiled. His smile grew as he stood up to introduce himself. They shook hands, and Gordon offered to show her where her next class was. She smiled back and accepted his offer. On the way to her next class Maggie and Gordon formed the start of an everlasting friendship. Maggie made Gordon laugh, and Gordon was the first solid guy Maggie had ever met. They soon became the best of friends, creating a jealousy that spread throughout their whole grade.

Maggie opened up her eyes and looked deeply into Pete's. "I don't know where to start."

Pete grinned, "Okay...then I'll ask the questions."

Maggie leaned back and waited.

"When is your birthday?" The first question came.

"January 14."

He nodded and asked another question, "Are you older or younger than Todd?"

"Younger."

"Okay." He paused, thinking of another question. "What town were you born in?"

Maggie thought for a long time. In her mind she started to think backwards. River Valley, New York City, here…I can't remember the last city. Looking up she took in a deep breath and said, "I don't know."

He laughed, "You don't know?"

She shook her head, "I really can't remember." She started to laugh along with him. It was the first time in days she had laughed, and it felt good. Maggie looked back at Pete, "Tell me something about you."

He looked at her intently, "There's not much about me…I moved here a few years ago, and I'll probably be living here my whole life."

That's what I thought. Maggie said to herself. *But look what happened.* She couldn't hold back the hatred that was forming against her father. Everything that he had done, all the lies that he had told. Maggie couldn't hold it in any longer. She felt a lump in her throat, and her head started to spin.

I want to go home. I can't live here anymore. The voices in her head started to consume her thoughts. *I want a normal life.* Maggie closed her eyes again. This time she remembered her mother. Todd was standing next to her, the two of them were only three. They were standing in the back yard of their first house. In the background, Maggie could hear music playing. Her parents were holding on to each other, spinning around in circles. Her mother was smiling. Todd reached over and grabbed onto Maggie's hand. The two of them started to run around in circles, giggling and jumping up and down.

Maggie brought herself back from the memory. Keeping her eyes closed she longed to have her family back. Maggie finally opened her eyes and looked back at Pete. He smiled. "You look like something is bothering you."

She slowly nodded. Maggie didn't like being very open with guys, but there was something about this one that pushed her towards telling him everything.

"Do you want to talk about it?"

Maggie was taken back by how caring his voice was. She thought it over for a moment, thinking of how she could ever explain these things to Pete. She decided she would only tell him the important things, and only when he asked. Maggie nodded her head and looked away.

"So what's on your mind?" He leaded forward, resting his elbows on his knees. Pete looked directly at Maggie, he watched carefully as her expressions slowly changed.

Maggie turned to face him. "I don't know where to start."

As she was talking, Pete reached over and took hold of her hand. Instead of pulling back like she normally would, Maggie smiled and tightened her grip.

A steady snow was falling around River Valley High. The night sky was broken up by millions of small white dots. Gordon smiled as he and Kailey hurried inside together. Gordon turned and waved their ride goodbye as he held open the door for Kailey to walk in. After adjusting to the warmth of the building, they followed the sound of music to the gym where a live DJ was singing to a small band behind him.

Gordon took Kailey's coat and offered to hang it up for her. She left him and went to join a group of her friends. By the time he got back Kailey had told them all that Gordon was going to go out with her. Ashley, one of Kailey's friends walked up to Gordon as he was coming back towards Kailey. She smiled at him, "So you've finally given up on Maggie?"

Gordon thought for a long time. He looked over at Kailey, she had a girlish smile on her face. Scanning the room for Delia he found her engaged in a deep conversation with Chris and Josh. Gordon looked back down at Ashley. He nodded his head and lied, "Yeah…I guess I have."

Chapter 18

After her afternoon spent with Pete, Maggie found herself doing a lot with him. He had become one of Todd's best friends, and Maggie often came home to find him in her house. She didn't mind it much. She would smile, walk off to her bedroom, and then join them a few minutes later. Often times she would accompany them on their visits downtown, where they met up with a few more of Pete's friends. The group of them would go hang out and talk. Most of the time Maggie was the only girl, but she didn't mind. She felt that she had only made friends with the guys at her school, and not too many of the girls.

It was the beginning of December and a light snow was falling down over the small town of Carison. Pete was walking with Maggie back to her house. Todd had fallen ill with a nasty cold, and had stayed home from school for his second day in a row. As they were walking, Pete reached his hand over and took Maggie's. She looked up at him in shock, but then smiled and moved closer to him.

He grinned down at her, "You've become more friendly lately." He stated slyly.

Maggie's smile grew bigger, "I guess I've changed a lot since I got here."

"I'll say," He said quickly, "I thought you were going to bite my head off the first time I met you."

Maggie looked away, slightly embarrassed, "I'm sorry...I was just having a bad day."

He squeezed her hand, "Well I'm glad you're back to your happy self again."

She smiled, "Me too."

When they got to Maggie's house they found that only Todd and Kevin were home. Todd was lying on the couch, he was covered up and looked pale. Kevin was sitting at his feet with a remote control in his hand. When Maggie walked in the room he looked up. "You two have to entertain me all night." He spoke in a snobbish voice.

Maggie looked over at Todd for an explanation. Todd shrugged, "Dad and Samantha are going on a 'date', he thinks they'll be gone until late tonight. We are suppose to watch the kid until he shuts up and goes to bed."

Kevin looked over at Todd, placing his hands on his hips he started to yell. "I don't talk all the time! I'm your little brother…you're suppose to be nice to me!"

Todd laughed, he sat up slowly, and stood up even slower. Finally he turned to face Kevin. "I'm not your brother…I don't have to be nice." The sentence ended abruptly, and Todd turned to leave. As he passed by Maggie he turned to her and said, "He's all yours."

Maggie forced a sarcastic smile, "Thanks." She looked up at Pete. "If you want to go now you can." She reluctantly said.

He shook his head, "As long as it is okay with you that I am here, then I'd love to stay."

"Thanks." She said as she let out a sigh of relief.

The two of them turned to face their nightmare.

Gordon was waiting for Kailey outside of the school library. It was almost three thirty, when they were suppose to meet. Gordon was going to take Kailey down to the lake to ice skate, and Kailey had insisted that they go directly from school.

He leaned against the wall and let his backpack fall to the floor. Letting out a huge sigh he closed his eyes and tried to focus his thoughts. When he opened them a blond-haired, medium height girl was standing in front of him.

He smiled, "Hey Delia…long time no chat."

Delia smiled back, "Yeah," she joined him in leaning against the wall, "it seems like since Maggie left, you and I haven't talked at all."

Gordon shrugged, "I guess not."

Delia lifted her left eyebrow. "Are you okay…is something wrong?"

He was silent.

Delia knew something was bugging him, "Do you want to talk about…"

She was interrupted by Kailey's voice coming from down the hall. She was walking quickly, letting her hair bounce behind her.

Gordon forced a smile to his lips. Kailey didn't notice anything wrong with him, she just took his hand and started to walk down the hall with him. Gordon looked back at Delia, he had a pleading look in his eyes. Delia smiled and mouthed the words 'call me'. He nodded and turned his attention back to Kailey.

"What should I do?" Gordon asked as he talked to Delia on the phone. "I just don't feel right anymore."

Delia tried to think of a reasonable answer. She let out a sigh, "Gordon, I'm not the right person to ask for advice…Maggie is remember?"

He winced, "I don't think I can ask her advice on this one." Gordon closed his eyes, he pictured Maggie's smile. *I miss her so much.* He told himself.

Delia was taken back by his words, "You use to be able to tell Maggie everything…what changed?"

He shrugged even though she couldn't see him, "Everything…I'm not the same person."

"I know you're not…and I don't like the new you. I know Maggie wouldn't either."

He nodded to himself, "I know, I know…but Delia…" he hesitated, "…can I be blunt with you?"

"Of course."

"I use to think that Maggie and I had something, she meant the world to me…I even told her that I loved her." He paused, remembering the day. "But she left me...and what we had isn't there anymore. There is no way it could work between us." Gordon's voice lost all of its feeling. He sounded like an emotionless machine, repeating something that it is suppose to say.

Delia had had it with him, "Gordon listen to yourself!" She screamed, "You...the person who always has hope, the encourager who can convince anyone that good things will come...you, Gordon Allister...listen to me! What you and Maggie had can't be taken away. There is no way that anyone or anything can ever take it away from you. Even if you are miles apart, and go separate ways. What was there will always be there...if you let it be there." She waited for a moment before continuing, "Don't you get what I am saying?" The tone of her voice had changed, and she started to sound more mature. Delia waited a long time before Gordon said anything.

"Yeah...I think I do." He finally said.

Maggie finally convinced Kevin to go up to bed. He did, after insisting that Maggie come tuck him in. She followed him up the steps, and into his room. He lay down on his bed and waited for Maggie to pull the covers up over him. She reached for them and tugged on them until they came all the way up. Patting the top cover down over his side she smiled and said goodnight. He repeated it and closed his eyes. Maggie left the room, turning off the light on her way out.

She walked down the steps and met Pete at the bottom. He took both of her hands and pulled her closer to him. Maggie stopped so she was less than a foot away from him.

He was grinning, "Do you want me to leave yet?" He asked slyly.

She shook her head. Maggie was about to step closer when the phone rang. For a brief second she leaned her head against his chest, not willing to let go and get the phone. But then she slowly backed away and walked towards the end table where one of the phones was sitting. Pete followed her and leaned against the side of the couch as he waited for her.

"Hello?" Maggie answered curiously.

"Maggie?" Gordon's deep voice rang from the other end.

Slowly Maggie backed up, there was a look of shock on her face. "Hi...hi Gordon." She finally said in a nervous voice.

At hearing the name, Pete took it as a sign and motioned to Maggie that he was leaving. Maggie smiled and waved goodbye with her free hand. He waved back and walked towards the door.

"How have you been?" Gordon asked, just as Pete was leaving.

Maggie was hesitant, "Pretty good...you?"

Gordon was even more hesitant, "Okay, I guess."

Maggie knew Gordon was holding something back, but she didn't know how to ask him what it was. She knew she could just come out and say it, but as she was talking to him, Maggie felt weird, like something was missing.

"Gordon..." She tried to say something, but he interrupted her.

"I'm sorry Maggie...I am so sorry."

Maggie was taken back at how honest his voice sounded. "Sorry about what?" She asked, partially confused.

"I don't know...I guess I just want to start over with you." Gordon let out a sigh, he had no idea how Maggie would respond, and as the seconds ticked by his heart started to pound harder.

"How?"

Those were not the words that Gordon expected. He waited a moment before saying, "I want things to be the way they use to be."

"Gordon...I just don't want to hold you back. I mean...a lot of people like you and would love to go out with you. I don't want to be the stupid girlfriend that lives miles away."

Gordon responded quickly, "Those people don't mean anything to me Maggie." He assured her, "They don't make me laugh, they don't make me happy, they don't know me inside and out. No one compares to you, and I don't want whatever we had all those years to go away just because you moved."

Maggie took in every word he said. After a long moment of thinking over what she was going to say, Maggie started to talk. "Gordon...can I tell you what I really want?"

"Yeah, you can tell me anything."

"Good." Maggie continued, "You and me...we're best friends...and I really like you. But I am so afraid that I'll lose you that I'm willing to put my feelings aside and just be your friend. Do you get what I'm saying?"

Gordon's heart sank. "Yeah, I think I get it. But where does it leave us?"

Maggie shook her head, "I don't know." She thought about it for a moment, "Maybe we are just suppose to remember each other as a good memory and get on with our lives."

Gordon answered quickly, "I'm not just going to forget about you."

Maggie was silent. She felt her throat swell up, and tears forming in her eyes. "Gordon..." A tear ran down her cheek. "Gordon...I don't want to live my life without you as my best friend. I want you to always be there for me." Maggie started to cry, it was a soft cry that Gordon could faintly hear.

"I'll always be there for you." He tried to assure her.

She shook her head, "You can't be...not when you're miles away." She paused to stop crying. "I want you to be there to give me hugs and to smile at me and to make me laugh." She tried to explain what she was feeling inside.

He took in a deep breath. "I'll always be here waiting for you."

Maggie heard a car pull into the driveway. She looked out the front window and saw her father getting out of the car. Quickly turning the other way she told Gordon she had to go, and hung up. Maggie hurried up to her room and closed the door. She fell onto her bed, burying her head into the stomach of her teddy bear. She felt her tears soaking up into its fur. After a few minutes she got up and changed into her pajamas and got herself ready for bed. Maggie walked over to her door and flipped off the light switch, walking back to her bed she got in it and tried to fall asleep.

Chapter 19

The next day at school Gordon explained to Kailey that he had been leading her on and he really didn't like her. She started to cry and turned away. Gordon felt bad, but also felt good at the same time. He met up with Delia in homeroom and told her about his conversation with Maggie the night before. Delia smiled, inside she knew that Maggie and Gordon were back to their normal selves again.

Gordon and Delia started to do things together. They would hang out after school, do big projects together and go over to each other's houses and talk. The town was now covered in snow and ice. Christmas was five days away, and school was on its last day before Christmas break.

"Hey Gordon!" Delia yelled from behind him as she tried to catch up with him.

He turned and around and gave her a welcoming smile.

"Got any plans for vacation?" She asked him as they started to walk again.

He shook his head, "You?"

"Nope..." she hesitated before finishing her sentence, "I talked to Maggie last night...she convinced her father to let her and Todd come visit for a while next week."

Gordon's face brightened up, "Really?"

Delia took in a deep breath, "Yeah, it took a lot of convincing, but they are flying in on Saturday."

Gordon smiled. It was times like these when he loved having Delia as a friend.

Maggie walked up her front steps and opened the door. Stepping inside her house she let the heat warm her up. As she was taking her shoes off she noticed her father and Samantha sitting on the couch. She turned to them in shock. "Why are you home?" She asked her father.

He smiled, "It's nice to see you too."

Maggie corrected herself and said hello, she then turned to Samantha and said hello to her too. After turning to hang her coat up she asked her question again.

He motioned for her to sit down. "Samantha and I would like to talk to you."

Maggie knew that it couldn't be good. She glanced around the room, hoping Todd would be home from school. But he wasn't. He and Pete had gone into town, suddenly Maggie was wishing that she had gone with them.

Taking in a deep breath she asked her father what was wrong.

Jacob looked over at Samantha and then back at Maggie, "We're concerned that you and Todd don't feel like a part of the family. We're afraid that you'll want to run away as soon as you can. And we'd like to prevent that."

Maggie nodded at each statement that he made.

"Maggie, we need your help in trying to make this family work. I know that you think you're not really a part of it anymore, but please try."

For a moment Maggie thought her father might be begging her to do something. But he continued.

"I know Todd has completely disconnected himself from us, and I don't want you to as well. Samantha and I have talked about it and we think it would be for the best if you and Todd don't go back to River Valley next week like you had planned."

Maggie couldn't believe what she was hearing. "You...you can't." She didn't know what to say. Instead of feeling hatred towards her father, Maggie suddenly found herself glaring at Samantha. *It's all her fault.* Inside of her head, Maggie started to blame everything on her.

"I'm sorry Maggie," she heard her father saying, "it's for the best."

Maggie slowly stood up. She was shaking her head. "No...no dad, you're wrong." With that she stormed up the steps and into her room. Maggie fell onto her bed. She reached over and grabbed the picture of her and Gordon off her bed stand, and stared at it for a long time.

Later that night she called Delia and told her they couldn't come. Delia called Gordon and broke the news to him, he was devastated.

Christmas that year came and went. Maggie and Todd became completely isolated from the rest of their family. Todd and Kevin got in more fights, and Maggie found herself following Todd out of the house more than once a week. The two of them would take long walks until it got extremely dark out, then they would head home and find everyone up in their beds.

"Maggie you can't live like this forever." Pete was trying to explain to her one day after school. The two of them were sitting in the school library, waiting for Todd to join them. It was the beginning of January, one of the first days back to school after the break.

Maggie thought about a reasonable answer. She knew he was right, but she didn't know how to explain to him what really went on in her house every night. "You don't know what it's like Pete." She tried to tell him.

He grinned, "You don't think I fight with my parents?" He asked her.

She nodded, "I know you do...but look at how differently our families are."

He disagreed, "They're not that different. My parents never divorced quite like yours did, and I don't have a half brother. That's really the only difference."

Maggie had forgotten that she never told Pete about her real mother. She had made up a story about Samantha being her real mother and her father had gone through a series of divorces with another woman before Kevin was born. Maggie took in a deep breath, she was beginning to regret that.

"Whatever." She said in a low voice. The two of them sat in silence until Todd walked up to them. Maggie stood up and joined her brother. Todd asked Pete if he wanted to come back to their house, but he declined.

"I think I'll go home today." He told them as he gathered his things. Maggie said a quiet goodbye and started to leave. Todd followed her and they started to walk home.

Once they were a small distance away from the school Todd asked, "What was that all about?"

Maggie explained to him how she had lied about their parents and it was coming back to haunt her.

Todd smiled, "That's okay." They walked the rest of the way in silence.

At home things got worse. Maggie found Kevin going through her stuff in her room. She blew up at him and screamed at him to get out of her room. Kevin ran away crying. Maggie picked up her things and went into Todd's room. She fell onto his bed and started to cry. He looked over from his computer chair.

"What's wrong?"

Between her cries she managed to explain everything to him, "I can't stand it here anymore. Dad has completely changed, Kevin is such a spoiled brat, and Samantha hates me just as much as mom did."

Todd got up from his chair and sat down next to her. He put his hand on her shoulder. "It's gonna be okay Maggie." He tried to assure her. As soon as he said the words the memories came. First it was the night they left, Maggie and Todd were hiding in the corner, listening to their parents fight. Next came the one when their mother slapped Maggie across the cheek. Todd hurried Maggie up the steps and into their room. The scene inside his mind changed again, this time it was a new one, and Maggie wasn't involved.

"Elise, I'm so glad you came back." A tall blond haired man was inviting Elise into an embrace at the airport. Todd was standing at

her side, looking up at the tall man. He leaned down and kissed Elise, Todd was tugging on her sleeve, trying to pull her away. Elise backed away and looked down at him. Todd expected her to smile, but instead she had an unpleasant look on her face. With a light shove she told him to go stand in the corner and wait for her. Todd willfully obeyed. He stood in that corner for two hours before Elise came back to find him half-asleep against the large observation window. She pulled him up and dragged him away, yelling at him for running off and not telling her where he went.

Todd shook himself out of his memory. It was then that he realized what Elise had done to him that day. He looked over at Maggie, she had stopped crying, but her face was still covered by her hands. Todd took in a deep breath, *It's time I fulfill my spot as 'big brother'*, he told himself. Todd reached over and picked up his phone. He dialed the number of the airline and waited for someone to answer.

The next day on the way home from school Todd cashed out his whole bank account. The amount was well over a few thousand dollars, but he figured they could use it all later. Maggie packed two bags full of the things they would definitely need, she wrote out a note explaining to their father that they were going home and he shouldn't worry about them. She wrote that it would be wise of him not to come and get them, and they would be coming back before the end of the month. Maggie left the note on the screen of her father's computer. The two of them were out of the house before Kevin got home from school.

Four and a half-hours later Todd and Maggie stepped off the plane and walked through the tunnel until they reached the terminal. Maggie smiled as she saw the familiar airport. Todd told her he was going to get their luggage, he turned and was off before she could say anything. As he walked away he had a grin on his face. *We did it.* He congratulated himself.

Maggie walked down the familiar aisles of the River Valley

airport. She briefly looked to her right and saw a young gentleman sitting with his head buried in his hands. She took no notice of him and continued to walk by. A few seconds later she heard her name.

"Maggie?"

Maggie instantly stopped. She slowly turned around to face the figure that was now standing. He was a tall, brown haired teenager, with a huge smile on his face. Maggie couldn't believe her eyes. She stood still and stared at him. Finally after a long time she took a small step forward.

Gordon's smile grew. He opened his arms and watched as Maggie ran into them. Wrapping his arms around her, Gordon held her close. Maggie leaned her head against his chest and smiled.

From a distance Todd's grin was growing as he watched his sister and Gordon be re-united.

Chapter 20

Maggie stepped back and looked up at Gordon. He smiled, "You came back."

Ignoring his comment, Maggie gave him a confused looked and asked, "How did you know?"

Gordon glanced over at Todd, who was watching them from a distance. "Your brother called me last night and told me when to come to the airport…so I came." He grinned.

Maggie couldn't help the smile on her face from growing. *What would I do without Todd?* She asked herself. Maggie turned to face her brother, who was walking towards them with all of their luggage dragging behind him. Maggie stepped forward and took hers from him. She smiled at him. He shook his head and chuckled.

"I've always wanted to run away." Todd commented just as Gordon asked how they convinced their father to let them leave. Todd repeated himself by saying they left a note and would probably get a phone call as soon as they got home. Gordon joined them in their laughing.

"I don't get how you two can get away with so much."

Maggie and Todd looked at each other, but Maggie was the one to answer. "Daddy really doesn't care. It's not like there's a money problem…and we're use to doing things by ourselves."

Gordon shook his head, "You guys are too much for me."

The three of them piled into Gordon's car and drove out of the parking lot. It was a sunny, but cold day. There was about a foot of snow on the ground, but the roads were clear. Maggie leaned against the back seat window and watched the houses pass by. She smiled. *I really missed this place.*

Gordon turned onto Maggie's old street and pulled into their driveway. It was partially covered in snow, and the house looked deserted. Maggie immediately opened the car door and jumped out. She hurried over to the front door and unlocked it.

Inside, the house was cold and dark. Maggie took a slow step forward. After another moment she walked over to the light switch and turned it on. The room came to life. Maggie walked into her study and turned on the lights. She smiled at the room she had come to love.

Todd walked in behind her. "Gordon had to leave, he said he might be back later."

Maggie nodded as Todd walked over and sat on the couch. "This place is freezing, where's the thermostat?"

Maggie shrugged, "I think it might be in dad's office."

Todd got up and walked out of the room. Maggie heard him open the door to their father's office. The house was completely quiet, she could hear his footsteps on the wooden floor as he walked around the room looking for the thermostat. Maggie stepped out of her study and walked towards the kitchen. Todd called her name as she was turning on another light. Maggie met him in the doorway of their father's study.

"What?"

He looked worried, "Maggie...what does dad do for a business?"

She shrugged, "He's just like the boss of a big company."

Todd walked into the room and pointed to a letter sitting on the end of the conference table. It was opened and looked like it had been sitting there for a while. "Does he deal with foreign countries?"

Maggie picked up the letter and scanned through it. The message was written in French.

Jacob,
Je ne suis pas plu de dire que nous ferons non plus long a fini des affaires avec vous. J'ai apprécié le passé dix années comme votre partenaire, mais après la mort di Elise je me sens que nous non plus

long a la connexion que nous avions. S'il vous plait acceptez mes exuses humbles comme je retire mes comtes de vos affairès . Je ne peux pas croire seulement quáprès toutes ces années vous trahiriez mon Samantha de confiance et contact encore. Elise serait décu, et je sais que je suis.
    Sincérement,
    Piere Meiblurle

    Maggie handed it to Todd and watched as he read through it. His eyes were constantly changing, and Maggie couldn't figure out if it was a bad or good letter. Finally Todd started to read it out loud, "Jacob, I am not pleased to say that we will no longer be doing business with you. I enjoyed the past ten years as your partner, but after Elise's death I feel that we no longer have the connection that we use to have. Please accept my humble apology as I withdraw my accounts from your dealings. I just cannot believe that after all these years you would betray my trust and contact Samantha again. Elise would be disappointed, and I know I am. Sincerely, Piere Meiblurle."

    Maggie sat down, she had a confused look on her face. "I don't get it."

    He shrugged, "Neither do I, it just doesn't sound like a normal friendly letter."

    Suddenly Maggie remembered something. She quickly left the room and ran into her study. Opening the top drawer of one of her desks she pulled out another letter. It was the one that Todd had found in the attic. Maggie looked at the signature at the bottom of the letter. She smiled and walked back into the office. Maggie pointed at the signature as she showed it to Todd.

    He nodded, "I guess they weren't enemies." Maggie sat down and compared the two letters. The first one was asking Elise to come back to France, the second one apologized for having to end business dealing with the guy who lost his wife. Maggie shook her head and handed them back to Todd. He re-read them both and shrugged. "You know him better than me." Todd reminded Maggie.

    She nodded in agreement, but then added, "But you were in

France...I wasn't."

Todd let out a sigh, "Maggie, mom was a dress designer. She went to work, sewed and came home. That's about as innocent as you can get."

Maggie was deep in thought, "What about this Piere guy, do you know who he is?"

Todd shook his head, "Nope. Mom and I hardly ever saw each other, we never talked."

Maggie's face began to lose hope. She looked around the room. "Did you ever find the thermostat?"

Todd lay awake in his bed. He stared at the ceiling and tried to remember, *It's so stupid,* he told himself, *why can't people be happy and not have to ruin other peoples' lives?* The questions started to run through his mind. He sat up and leaned against his wall. Todd closed his eyes, *Mom was always hiding something...what was it?* He tried to remember.

The door opened, Maggie walked in and noticed Todd sitting up in his bed. "You couldn't sleep either?" She asked as she sat down next to him.

He shook his head, "None of this makes any sense. I just don't get it."

Maggie leaned her head against Todd's shoulder. "Todd, why did you and mom move back to France?"

He thought about it for a long time. "I really don't know. I always thought it was because they just couldn't get along. But it might have been because there was another guy waiting for her, and now it looks like dad might have come up with the idea himself."

Maggie felt herself growing extremely tired, "What do you remember about the night she left?"

Todd closed his eyes, it all came back to him again. Maggie and Todd were sitting in the living room, watching TV when Elise walked in. She smiled at Todd and then looked over at Maggie. A tear came to her eye but she quickly covered it up by yelling at Maggie to go upstairs. Maggie quickly ran out of the room, but was stopped by her father who grabbed hold of her arm and pulled her into the kitchen area. Elise was holding onto both of Todd's shoulders, telling him something.

Jacob looked at her intently, she tried to force a smile, but found herself ready to cry again. Elise looked down at Maggie, "I noticed you didn't make your bed today." She started to say.

Jacob gave her a sharp glare, "Elise, she's only five. Did you make your bed when you were five?" He challenged her in a calm voice.

"Jacob I don't want to start this again. It's hard enough already…please…not in front of the children." A tear ran down her face.

"They'll have to know the truth eventually…when are we going to explain it to them?"

Elise shrugged, "I don't want to do this."

Jacob tried to force a smile, "You have to…I still love you Elise." Quickly, Elise turned and walked towards the door.

"I don't know why I ever got myself into this mess." She opened the door and walked out, holding onto Todd's wrist, "Goodbye Jacob!" She screamed as she shut the door and headed for the car.

Todd opened his eyes. "They didn't hate each other Maggie."

She raised her head from his shoulder. "How do you know?"

Todd turned his head to face her, "I don't know why she had to leave, but she didn't want to, and she certainly didn't hate you."

Maggie closed her eyes, "Then why did she always yell at me?"

The flashbacks came to Todd again. But this time there was more. "Maggie, I don't think you remember, but I do. She never yelled at you until a few months before we moved away. She knew she would never see you again, and the only way she knew how to hide the pain she was feeling, was to yell." Todd put his arm around his sister. "I'm going to call dad tomorrow and tell him that we're going to stay for a while and that he shouldn't worry about us."

Maggie nodded, closed her eyes and quickly fell asleep.

Chapter 21

Maggie woke up and found herself lying under the covers of Todd's bed. She smiled and turned to see him sitting at his desk. There was a pillow and a blanket lying on his floor. Maggie watched him for a minute. *He does a lot for me*, she finally realized. Todd was reading an email on the computer. Maggie couldn't tell who it was from, but he seemed to be concentrating extremely hard.

Todd looked over and saw Maggie watching him, he smiled. "Good morning."

Maggie looked at the computer screen, "Who's that from?" She asked.

He hesitated for a moment, "One of my friends from back home." Maggie got up and walked over behind him. She glanced over the letter. The whole thing was written in French. *That is really going to get annoying.* She told herself and she sat back down on his bed. He was watching her, "What do you want to do today?"

Maggie shrugged, "We should probably call dad."

Todd nodded, "I don't want to wake him, so I'm going to wait a while." He waited for a moment. "Gordon called a little while ago, he said that he and Delia are gonna stop by for a while."

Maggie smiled. Standing up she told Todd she was going to get ready.

After her shower, Maggie met Todd downstairs. He was reading the back of the cereal box as he scooped the flakes into his mouth. As Maggie walked up he said, "I really do hate English, it's so stupid, nothing makes sense."

Maggie laughed and poured a bowl for herself. "Well, I'm not all that fond of you having conversations with people, and me not being able to know what you're saying."

It was Todd's turn to laugh. He shook his head and continued to eat his breakfast. After both of them were done, Maggie suggested that they go call their father. The two of them went into Maggie's study and Todd made the call.

Jacob answered the phone immediately, he already knew who it was. "Todd, what were you two thinking?" He yelled.

Todd didn't answer.

"You had me and Samantha worried sick!" He continued to yell, "I want the two of you to come home right away!"

This time Todd did answer, "No."

"What?"

"I said 'no'. We're not coming home." Todd spoke firmly.

The door opened, Gordon and Delia walked in. Maggie ran over and hugged Delia. Todd smiled from where he was standing.

"I won't have you talking back to me Todd. Now I want you and Maggie to come home today!"

"Look, dad, just give us a week or two. We'll come back, don't worry. We just need some time."

Mr. Morgan thought about it for a long time. When he spoke his voice was quieter and he stopped yelling. "I want the two of you home next Saturday. If you're not there then I'm coming down to get you."

Todd smiled and let out a deep breath, "Thanks, dad."

The two of them hung up and Todd turned to face the others. Maggie waited for him to say something. After a long moment he did, "We got 'till next Saturday."

Maggie jumped up excitedly. She ran forward and hugged her brother, then went back and hugged Delia. Delia put her hands on Maggie's shoulders and calmed her down.

"Maggie...breathe!"

Maggie stopped jumping and smiled.

Gordon started to laugh, "Maggie, you only have a week."

Maggie's eyes widened, "You're right. Let's go do something."

She took his hand and pulled him out of the room.

Todd grinned at Delia as she started to laugh. Delia turned around and sat down. Todd slowly walked over and sat down next to her. He turned to face her. "So, how have you been?"

Delia ignored his question, "How come you only told Gordon you were coming back?" She smiled.

Todd played along, "Because he has a car." He grinned. "I missed you." Delia's cheeks grew red, and Todd's grin got bigger.

Delia stayed silent as Todd watched her. After a moment she spoke, "School's just not the same without you."

Todd smiled, "We'll be back soon." He assured her.

She gave him a confused look. "How?"

"I don't know, but we're not going to be going back on Saturday, I just haven't figured how yet."

Delia smiled, "So you're really going to stay?"

The next day was Sunday, Maggie and Todd woke up early again and were met an hour later by Delia. She told them that Gordon was at church and he would come around noon. This time the three of them walked around the town. They spent an hour at the coffee shop, and another hour watching a hockey game that was being played on the frozen harbor. Around eleven thirty the three of them walked back to Todd and Maggie's house. There they sat around talking until Gordon showed up. He was wearing a nice light blue shirt and beige pants.

Todd snickered as he walked in, but Delia stopped him before he said anything.

Gordon sat down and waited for someone to say something.

Finally Maggie spoke, "Todd, can you ice skate?"

As Todd finished tying his skates, Maggie explained the rules. She was standing on the edge of their pond, testing out her skates on the ice. "Me and Delia, against Todd and Gordon. We are shooting that way," She said as she pointed to the far net, "And you guys are shooting that way." She pointed to the other side. "Rules are pretty basic…we play until my team wins." Laughing, Maggie and Delia skated out on the ice and waited for the other two. Gordon met Maggie near the center, and Todd dropped the puck. The game had begun.

Quickly Gordon took the puck and passed it to Todd, who quickly skated down the ice with it. Delia met up with him and stole the puck away. She passed it to Maggie, who took a shot on Gordon, who was now standing in the net. He blocked her shot and then passed it to Todd, who attempted to move the puck further down the ice. Delia intercepted him and laughed as he fell flat on his face. He quickly got back up and chased Delia down the ice. She had passed the puck to Maggie, who was shooting again on Gordon. This time he missed, and the puck flew into the net. Maggie threw her stick up in victory and proclaimed that it was one to nothing.

Gordon retrieved the puck and started down the ice with it. He cleverly skated around Maggie and met up with Delia at the net. He held the puck there for a long time, waiting for the right moment to shoot. Todd skated up a few feet away from Gordon. Gordon pretended to pass the puck to Todd, but instead he made the shot, and watched as the puck flew right past Delia. It was their turn to brag.

Delia passed the puck to Maggie, who skated down the ice, she was about to pass it again when Todd stole it away. Delia started to guard Todd, so Maggie headed down towards the net. Gordon now had possession of the puck, he hit the puck hard with his stick at the same time Maggie was turning around to face him. The puck flew through the air. Gordon saw what was happening and yelled at Maggie to get out of the way. But she didn't hear him in time. The puck hit her right next to her left eye, and slightly below the center of her temple. Maggie fell onto the ice, Gordon quickly skated up to her and found her unconscious. He fell to his knees, and held onto Maggie's shoulders, watching as blood poured out of the cut next to her eye.

Chapter 22

Todd, Delia and Gordon were sitting in the emergency room when Mr. Morgan rushed in. Todd had called him right after calling the ambulance, and he had immediately bought a ticket and flew over. It had been almost five hours, but the doctor still hadn't said anything about Maggie.

After giving Todd a quick hug, Jacob walked up to the front desk. The receptionist smiled at Mr. Morgan's familiar face.

"How are you today?" She asked him in a cheerful voice.

He frowned, "Terrible." He said harshly.

The woman looked shocked, "What can I do to help you?"

He put both of his hands on the counter and leaned forward. "I want to know how my daughter is doing." He demanded.

The woman began to type. "Maggie, right?"

Jacob nodded.

She continued, "I'm sorry," she looked up at him, "she's in ICU, and I can't tell you anything until the doctor lets me know."

Jacob gripped both of his hands together and took a deep breath. After letting his breath out he backed away from the counter. Turning around he slowly walked back to the three teenagers. Mr. Morgan sat down next to Todd and leaned back in the seat.

"Todd..."

Todd interrupted him before he could continue. "Don't say it dad, I know. We should have stayed there and none of this would have happened." Todd took in a breath, "I'm sorry I let this happen."

Jacob looked over at his son. He watched Todd for a long time. Todd was leaning back in his chair, staring off into space. His face looked tired from sitting around all day, and his eyes looked stressed out. Mr. Morgan finally realized how much responsibility Todd had taken on since he had moved over from France. "No Todd, I'm sorry." Todd looked up in surprise. "I should have talked it over with you two, and I should have never acted the way I did while we were in Nevada. I pushed you two away, and it's my fault that this all happened."

Mr. Morgan rubbed his eyes, "I guess I have a lot of explaining to do to you two, but I'll wait until we find out about Maggie."

Jacob didn't say anything else until the receptionist called his name fifteen minutes later. He walked up, anticipating what the woman had to say. She smiled, "Follow me."

Mr. Morgan walked through the door and followed the woman down the hall. They walked down a long hallway and then turned the corner. There they met up with the doctor. He stuck out his hand and introduced himself, "Mr. Morgan, I'm Dr. Jayson, it's nice to meet you."

Mr. Morgan accepted his greeting with a smile.

Dr. Jayson talked as he led Mr. Morgan around another corner, "Your daughter has experienced major head injuries. She was hit right between the eye and temple, and was knocked unconscious instantly." Dr. Jayson opened a door and motioned for Mr. Morgan to walk in. "She woke up a few minutes ago and she will be going in for tests soon. But I thought you might want to see her first."

"Thank you." He said as he walked forward into the dark room.

Maggie was lying on the bed with her eyes closed. Her hand had an IV line connected to it, and she had oxygen tubes connected to her nose. On the tip of her finger was a small, white clip. It gave off a carbon dioxide reading every two minutes. On the opposite arm was a band for reading blood pressure that gave off a number every minute. Next to her bed was a monitor. It beeped every two seconds, and showed her pulse rate on a screen.

Maggie's head was bandaged up. She had a large white bandage that went from her ear to right above her eye, covering part of it. It was the thickest right above her temple.

When the door opened Maggie opened her eyes and slightly turned her head. She smiled at her father. "Daddy." Her voice cracked.

He walked up and grabbed her hand. "I love you Maggie."

Maggie didn't pay attention to what he was saying. "I'm sorry Daddy. I'm so sorry."

Jacob squeezed her hand tighter, "Don't be honey. I don't want to talk about it now. I'm just glad that you are okay." He smiled down at his daughter.

Maggie yawned and closed her eyes. "I love you daddy." She said right before she fell asleep.

A few minutes later Dr. Jayson and another doctor came and rolled Maggie into a different room. There they performed a number of tests on her brain, and the tissue around her cut. After an hour of testing they rolled her back into her room and said she could receive visitors, only she would be tired for the next few hours.

While Todd, Delia and Gordon were talking to Maggie, Dr. Jayson pulled Mr. Morgan aside and said, "Mr. Morgan, we've checked over her brain, and she appears to be okay. It doesn't appear that she has lost any major memory, but a few things will more than likely be forgotten."

Mr. Morgan nodded.

"I want to keep her here for a few days." He continued, "About a week, to make observations and to be sure she is okay."

Again, Jacob nodded in agreement.

"Now, the cut by her eye..." He started. "I don't know for sure, but it will more than likely leave a scar. Not very big, but there will probably be one at the end of her eyebrow."

Mr. Morgan smiled, "As long as she is okay."

The doctor grinned, "I'm sure she'll be okay."

"So Gordon," Todd said into the receiver, "Maggie's been asking about you. Why haven't you been down to see her?"

Gordon shrugged, "I don't know."

Todd wouldn't accept that as an answer, "Yeah you do. Gordon what has gotten into you?" Todd questioned him again.

Gordon was silent for a long time.

"Just tell me Gordon, what is it?" Todd tried to get Gordon to speak.

Gordon took in a deep breath, "I can't." He said bluntly.

"Why?" Todd yelled into the receiver.

"Because I was the one that put her in the hospital. She doesn't want to see me."

Todd couldn't believe what he was hearing, "Gordon, listen to yourself." His voice was harsh. "The girl you love is there waiting for you, and that is the only excuse you can come up with?"

Gordon thought for a long time, finally he grinned and said, "You're right, I'll go tonight."

Todd smiled and hung up. He fell down onto his bed and closed his eyes. *Why? Why did everything have to change?* Todd fell asleep thinking of how he could change what was beginning to happen.

Two days had passed since the accident. Dr. Jayson had Maggie moved into a normal room as soon as they found out she was stable. Mr. Morgan had called up Samantha and asked her and Kevin to fly down for a few days. They came that afternoon.

The next day Gordon came to see Maggie. He opened the door and walked slowly up to her bed. She was half laying-half sitting on her bed, reading a book.

When the door opened she set the book down and looked to see who it was. The cut above her eye had started to heal. She wasn't wearing the large bandage anymore, but she still had the stitches in. The wound was still swollen, and had a black and blue circle around it.

Gordon tried to smile as he walked in. "Hey." He said quietly.

Maggie's face started to glow, she smiled back.

Gordon walked up to her bed and stood next to her. She looked up, "What took you so long?" She said with a growing smile on her face.

Gordon finally calmed down, a huge smile formed at the corners of his lips. "The nurse held me up at the front counter, she said I was too sexy to let you see me."

Maggie laughed, "You wish."

He sat down, "Yeah, it's my greatest desire to be that sexy."

Maggie pointed to her head, "I knew it." She said while letting a long waited for laugh find its way out of her.

Gordon stopped joking, "It's good to see you again."

Maggie let her normal smile take over. She looked into Gordon's brown eyes. "I missed you."

Gordon stayed and talked to Maggie for another hour. After a while Maggie started to get tired and Gordon left her so she could sleep.

Todd knocked on the door of his father's study. A voice called for him to come in, and Todd did. Jacob smiled as Todd walked through the door. "Hello son."

Todd returned his smile.

"What's up?" His father asked.

Todd sat down in front of his desk and looked at him intently. "I want you to tell me about mom."

Mr. Morgan was caught off guard. He looked at Todd and took in a deep breath. "What about her?"

Todd was about to say "everything", but he stopped himself and said, "Why did she have to leave?"

Jacob closed his eyes, "I guess it's time I tell you." He took in another deep breath and started his story. "Long before I met Elise I received a letter in the mail. I was fresh out of school, and this letter had a lot of promise in it. It said that there was an offer for me in Paris, and that I would become a world known figure if I took it up. Naturally, I did. I moved to France and met this man named Piere Mieblurle. He was only a year older than me, but he had many connections and hooked me up with all of them before the end of my first week there."

Todd interrupted, "What did you do?"

Mr. Morgan laughed, "Nothing. They told me that they just needed someone to be the boss of a new company that they were going to start."

Todd gave him a confused look. Jacob chuckled. "Sounds too good doesn't it?"

Todd nodded.

"It was. After a month they started to control my life. They knew everything I did, and if they didn't approve of something they would make a comment about it and threaten to take away my job if I didn't stop."

"What happened?" Todd started to get into his father's story.

Jacob grinned, "I talked to Piere about it one day, and he agreed with me that something had to be done. He told me that he had a plan on how to overthrow them, but still keep the company."

"Why did you want to keep the company?"

"Todd," he started, "I was only 22 and already making millions and famous. Would you want to get rid of a company that good?" He challenged.

Todd laughed at himself, "I guess not."

Mr. Morgan continued, "I thought that Piere's plan was just to buy them out, or to secretly transfer the company. But a few weeks later I read in the newspaper that the majority of Piere's connections had been murdered."

Todd's jaw dropped, "How can one guy get away with that many murders?"

Mr. Morgan shook his head, "You didn't let me finish. The rest of the connections had helped him, and they had done it secretly over a period of two weeks. No one suspected Piere or even me because Piere made it look like we were also targets, but were the lucky ones that got away."

Todd's eyes widened, "This is so cool." He kept shaking his head in astonishment. "So what happened next?"

Jacob leaned forward and stared his son in the eye. "The company took off, we were making twice as much and didn't have to worry about anyone watching us, or telling us what to do. Everything was good for about a year. Then one night at a dance club Piere introduced me to his fiancé."

Todd grinned, "You mean mom?"

Jacob smiled at his son, "Yes. That night Piere got extremely drunk and I offered to drive him and Elise home. I dropped off Piere, and started to drive Elise home. But instead of directions to her house, Elise gave me the directions to a small out of the way cabin. I figured she wanted me to drop her off there, but she asked me to stay."

The corners of Todd's lips started to form a smile.

"Let's just say I never got home that night." Jacob tried to hide his grin.

Todd smirked, "Then what happened?"

Jacob's cheeks turned red, "Elise was pregnant." He paused, "We worked out a plan, and figured out that if we both moved to America at different times he would never figure it out."

Todd was shaking his head, "Dad, guys are smarter than that."

Mr. Morgan laughed, "Not me." He continued, "I told Piere that I wanted to expand the company into America. He agreed and said that he would supply me with everything I needed to start the company. I moved to America and started the company. Elise broke up with Piere and disappeared the next day. The only person who knew where she went was her butler Geames."

Todd smiled at the memory of Geames.

"We re-united and got married before she was two months pregnant. No one ever knew, and Piere didn't figure it out until three years later. When he figured it out he sent a letter to Elise. Telling her that he was always waiting for her if she ever wanted to come back. Then he sent a letter to me telling me that if I didn't get rid of Elise he was going to get rid of me the same way he had gotten rid of all those other guys."

Todd leaned forward, his eyes started to widen again.

"I showed Elise the letter, and she agreed that she would eventually have to leave me. Elise flew to Paris and had a talk with Piere. She told him how she didn't want to leave you and Maggie. Piere pretended to understand and let it go for almost two more years. When you and Maggie were four Piere called me and gave me the first of many threats. After many hours on the phone and a lot of arguing, Piere told me he wanted Elise back and that was the end of the discussion. A week later he flew to America and introduced me to Samantha. Elise said that maybe Maggie wouldn't remember her, and that you wouldn't remember me. That way Maggie could think Samantha was her real mother, and you could think Piere was your father."

Todd gave his father all of his attention.

"After Elise left me Piere called to say that we were still friends and he hoped the company would continue to grow at the rate it was. I got really mad at him and told him that the only way we would stay friends and partners would be because of Elise. He agreed, and we went our separate ways." Jacob paused and took in a deep breath. "The company continued to grow, Samantha and I got married and had Kevin. Everything was good until I got another call from Piere. He told me he wanted me to start another company in New York City. I agreed, but Samantha didn't want to move. So we got a divorce because I didn't want to risk the company.

"Maggie and I moved to New York. Piere didn't bother us again until she was thirteen. Then he told me that he wanted another company in a small town called River Valley. I asked him why, but he just told me to go do it. So I did."

Todd gave his father another confused look, "Why?"

Jacob shrugged, "I didn't want to loose the company."

Todd shook his head in disgust.

Jacob continued, "Maggie and I were fine until the day I found out that Elise had died. I thought everything would be okay between Piere and me, but he remembered what I said all those years ago."

"What did you say?" Todd tried to remember.

"I said that I didn't want to be his partner or friend unless Elise was there. So when Elise died he told me that he didn't think it would work anymore. We tried to keep the company going, but three months ago the partnership was terminated."

Todd's jaw dropped again, "So what happened to the company?"

"He owns everything in Europe, and I own everything in the States." Jacob smiled, "It actually worked out very well."

Todd leaned back in his chair, "That's the whole story?"
Jacob nodded, "And the truth."

That Saturday Maggie was allowed to go home. She still had stitches but other than that no one could tell she had ever been hurt. The doctor said there would definitely be a scar, but it didn't bother Maggie. Her father signed her out of the hospital and drove her home. They didn't say anything the whole ride. Maggie was afraid they would have to go back to Nevada, and she didn't want to get in another fight with her dad.

When they got home Todd, Gordon, Delia and Kevin were eating pizza in the kitchen. Mr. Morgan joined in right away. After his first bite he motioned for Maggie to sit down. She sat on the stool next to Gordon and looked around. Finally she turned to her father, "Where's Samantha?"

Her father grinned. Gordon pulled her stool closer and put his arm around her waist. "Didn't they tell you?" He smiled as he looked down at her, "Samantha flew back to pack up her things, you're moving back here."